THE STALKER RETURNS, , , ,

A bolt of lightning sent long shadows across Selena's room.

Maybe I should forget homework and go to bed early, she thought.

She settled back on the bed as lightning crashed and rain thundered against the Fear Street Woods behind her house.

And then she heard something over the noise of the storm.

The thud of heavy footsteps. Footsteps in her house.

Selena's breath caught in her throat. She sat up in bed, her heart hammering in terror.

What if it was the stalker?

She tried not to hear the rhythmic sounds. *Thump . . . thump . . . scrape.*

The footsteps came closer. Someone was on the stairway. Someone was in the house.

Scrape . . . scrape . . . thump.

Closer. Almost at the top of the stairs now.

Silently, Selena slid off her bed. She unplugged her reading lamp. Grasped it by the base. Felt its weight in her hand.

Then she stepped behind the door and waited.

Look for more
heart-stopping stories from

FEAR STREET

The Beginning

The Perfect Date

Runaway

FEAR STREET

SECRET ADMIRER

R.L. STINE

SIMON PULSE

NEW YORK   LONDON   TORONTO   SYDNEY   NEW DELHI

SIMON PULSE

An imprint of Simon & Schuster Children's Publishing Division

1230 Avenue of the Americas, New York, New York 10020

First Simon Pulse paperback edition March 1996

This Simon Pulse paperback edition February 2021

Text copyright © 1996 by Parachute Press, Inc.

Cover illustration copyright © 2021 by Marie Bergeron

All rights reserved, including the right of reproduction in whole or in part in any form.

SIMON PULSE and colophon are registered trademarks of Simon & Schuster, Inc.

FEAR STREET is a registered trademark of Parachute Press, Inc.

For information about special discounts for bulk purchases, please contact Simon & Schuster Special Sales at 1-866-506-1949 or business@simonandschuster.com.

The Simon & Schuster Speakers Bureau can bring authors to your live event. For more information or to book an event contact the Simon & Schuster Speakers Bureau at 1-866-248-3049 or visit our website at www.simonspeakers.com.

Cover designed by Heather Palisi

Interior designed by Tom Daly

The text of this book was set in Excelsior LT Std.

Manufactured in the United States of America

10 9 8 7 6 5 4 3 2 1

This book has been cataloged with the Library of Congress.

ISBN 978-1-5344-8766-6 (pbk)

ISBN 978-1-4391-1552-7 (eBook)

PROLOGUE

Dear Selena,
Your name means "moon." Like the
moon, you are pale, beautiful, and
mysterious. Your blond hair is silvery
like the moon's rays.
Everyone admires you. Everyone
applauds for you.
I'm in your audience too, Selena.
Though I see you every day, you don't
see me. But someday that will change.
Someday I will be the only person in
your audience.
It will be just you and me, Selena.
Someday.
Someday very soon.
Yours forever,
The Sun

1

*H*e'll never hurt you again. I promise. He'll never hurt you again." Selena Goodrich's last words were almost a whisper.

The audience began to clap. Slowly the curtain came down, closing off the stage. Then it rose again.

Selena stepped to the front of the stage, smiling as she gazed out over the audience. Accepting the cheers and applause.

She bowed deeply, her blond curls tumbling over her shoulders. Then she straightened and turned to the other actors in the cast. She joined hands with Alison Pearson and Jake Jacoby, and the line of actors—everyone in the play—bowed together. The audience leaped to its feet, cheering loudly.

All these people came to see me, Selena thought in wonder. *I belong on the stage. Finally I know where I fit in.*

The curtain sank for the final time. Selena turned to her friends. "You were both terrific," she told them.

"Thanks, Selena," Alison murmured. Alison was pretty, with emerald eyes and long, straight black hair. She smiled at Selena. "But I'll never be as good as you. You were awesome!"

"Hey—you weren't bad, Moon," Jake added, punching Selena lightly on the shoulder. Of all her friends, he was the only one who still called Selena by her childhood nickname. He loved to tease her, and he knew the nickname annoyed her. Most other people didn't even know that "Selena" meant "moon."

"You weren't so bad yourself. At least you didn't fall on your face this time," Selena replied, rolling her eyes. "Are you going to the cast party?"

Jake shrugged. "I don't know," he said. "I'm not really psyched for a party."

Even through the stage makeup, Selena could see that Jake had dark circles under his eyes. She was about to ask him if anything was wrong when the drama club director swept between them.

"Congratulations, Selena!" he called out. "Tonight's performance was excellent. I love that thing you did with the handkerchief in the last act. You surprised even me!"

"Thank you, Mr. Riordan," Selena replied with a smile.

The handsome, gray-haired teacher stepped onto a riser and shouted for attention. "I'll see all of you at my house for the party!" he called over the buzz of voices. "But before we go, I want to remind you about tryouts next week for the spring play. You'll be happy to hear that we're doing a classic— *Romeo and Juliet*."

This news was greeted with a mixture of groans and cheers.

Romeo and Juliet! Selena thought with excitement. *I'll get a chance to do Shakespeare on stage!*

She hurried to her locker, pushing through the loud, happy crowd of actors backstage.

"Yo, Selena!" Danny Morris called. "Good job! You were cool!"

"Thanks," Selena replied curtly. She pushed past the stocky blond senior. Catching the disappointment on his tanned face, she felt the tiniest pang of guilt. *Maybe I should be nicer to Danny,* she thought.

After all, we meant something to each other . . . once. A long time ago.

These days, Selena couldn't figure out why all the girls at Shadyside High found Danny so fascinating.

She still couldn't believe she'd gone out with him for as long as she did. How had she been able to stand his showing off and selfishness for six whole months?

"Trying out for the spring play?" Danny demanded, stepping in front of her to block her path.

"Of course I am." Selena sighed. She tried to move around him, but he refused to budge. "Danny, listen, I'm in kind of a hurry—"

"You'll get to play Juliet for sure," Danny persisted, ignoring her attempts to get past. "Guess which part I'm trying out for."

"The castle pest?" Selena cracked.

"Selena!"

Selena turned at the familiar voice of her best friend, Katy Jensen. Katy came hurrying over in her stagehand's black coveralls.

"Later," she told Danny as Katy approached.

"You were excellent!" Katy gushed. "Even better than last night." She gave Selena a quick hug.

"Everyone hit it perfectly tonight," Selena told her friend. "It's like it all finally came together. And everything backstage went perfectly."

Katy wiped her forehead with the back of her hand. Her short, straight black hair stood on end. Her pale, round face shone with sweat in the dim backstage lights.

"I had a problem with the lights," she commented. "Didn't you notice?"

"Not at all," Selena replied.

"One of the spots became unfocused," Katy explained. "I rushed up there as soon as I saw it." She pointed to the catwalk that stretched high above the stage.

Selena glanced up and shuddered. *How could anyone have the nerve to climb up there?* she wondered. Just the sight of the narrow metal ladder built into the wall made her feel dizzy.

But Katy never seemed to mind heights. Even when they were little kids, she had been the one to climb trees while Selena cowered on the ground.

I guess that's why Katy likes being on the stage crew, Selena thought absently. She pulled open the door of the big locker room.

It was crowded with her friends from the play. While the play was in progress, this room doubled as the girls' dressing room. "I don't know why we even bother with lockers," Katy commented. "None of them lock anyway."

Selena shrugged.

"So are you ready for your next role?" Katy asked.

"What do you mean?" Selena demanded as she exchanged grins with Alison, who was also trying to push through the crowd of students.

"Come on." Katy laughed. "You know you'll get Juliet."

"Everyone keeps saying that," Selena declared. "But it's not like there's a guarantee I'll get the part."

Katy snorted. "Yeah, well, there's no guarantee the sun will rise tomorrow. But everyone knows you're perfect for Juliet. I mean, it's the last play of the year. No one will come if you aren't the star."

"Yeah, right!" Selena rolled her eyes.

Why did Katy always have to exaggerate everything? "Anyway, it's up to Mr. Riordan," she added.

"What's up to me?" Mr. Riordan approached the girls.

"We're talking about casting for the spring play," Selena told him.

Mr. Riordan nodded. "Casting for this next play might be particularly important," he confided.

"Why?" Katy asked.

"Well, it's supposed to be a secret, but . . . I just found out that the drama coach from Northwestern University will be here," Mr. Riordan whispered.

"You're kidding!" Selena gasped. Northwestern had one of the best drama departments in the country.

"I'm serious," he told her. "Each year he visits

different schools in the area to check out the talent. This year he has chosen Shadyside High."

"Whoa!" Selena cried. "I'm applying to Northwestern. But there's no way I can go without a scholarship."

"Then this is your big chance," Mr. Riordan said with a wink. He turned and headed for the stage door. "See you girls at the party."

"You never told me you wanted to go away to college," Katy remarked.

"Well, sure I *want* to," Selena replied. "But it's only a dream. I mean, Mom doesn't even make enough money to send me to the junior college."

"If that drama coach sees you play Juliet, he'll give you the scholarship," Katy predicted.

"That would be amazing," Selena replied. "But I'll believe it when I see it."

Most of the other students had cleared out. Selena yanked open the door of her locker. Her backpack hung on the hook where she'd left it.

But leaning against the pack, she saw something new—a large bouquet, wrapped in bluestriped paper.

"What is it?" Katy asked, gazing over Selena's shoulder.

"Cool!" Selena exclaimed. "Someone left me flowers! I wonder who?"

"Open them!" Katy urged.

Selena carefully pulled out the wrapped bouquet.

She ripped the paper from the top and peered inside.

And then she gasped in open-mouthed horror.

2

Selena dropped the bundle and stared down at it in shock.

Both girls gaped as the black, dead roses tumbled onto the floor.

"How gross!" Katy cried, pressing her hands against her cheeks.

"Yuck. Dead flowers," Selena groaned. "That's so sick."

And then she noticed a small white envelope shoved under the rubber band holding the limp stems together. She bent down and snatched it up. With trembling fingers, Selena pulled a typed note from it and read:

> *Dear Selena,*
> *Congratulations!*
> *Enjoy your last curtain call.*

*Did you know you are giving up the
stage—to be with me?
Forever.*

Selena stood frozen, staring down at the black bouquet. Her disappointment quickly turned to anger. "What a sick thing to do!" she exclaimed.

Katy held her nose against the foul odor of decay. "Why would anyone do this?"

Selena scanned the note again. "Look at this." She pointed to the bottom of the paper. There was no signature, only a bright orange sticker shaped like the sun. Selena scratched at it with her fingernail.

"What's that supposed to mean?" Katy asked.

Selena shrugged. "It's just a sticker. The kind that little kids collect."

"But why is it on the note?" Katy persisted.

"Who knows?" Selena snapped. "Who cares?" Holding her breath, she picked up the ugly bouquet and dumped it in the trash can in the corner of the room. "It's just a dumb joke."

"A *joke*?" Katy cried. "Are you crazy? What kind of person would think dead flowers are funny?"

"Someone with a really warped sense of humor," Selena replied. "Someone like . . . Jake!"

"Huh? Jake?"

"He's been playing tricks on me ever since we were little."

"Maybe," Katy agreed. "But this isn't his style. Besides, I don't think Jake is in the mood for jokes."

"Why not?"

"Haven't you noticed?" Katy replied. "Jake's been so weird lately! Tonight he went ballistic just because I asked him to hand me a prop."

"You know, he did look tired," Selena agreed. "I wonder what's up with him." She thought about it as she followed her friend out to the parking lot. Katy's car was parked under a tall oak tree.

"I still think Jake sent the flowers," Selena announced as they approached the darkened car. "I'll ask him about it later."

Selena shivered as she waited for Katy to open the car door. It was a chilly, overcast night, and the tree branches whipped in the wind as if they were dancing.

"I hope it *was* Jake," Katy said, pulling her keys from her jacket pocket. "But that note sounds like it could be from someone really messed up."

As Katy pulled out of the parking lot, Selena's thoughts were already racing with ideas about the spring play. She could imagine how she'd begin her audition, which scenes she wanted to learn. . . .

"Earth to Selena." Katy's voice interrupted her thoughts. "Are you still with us?"

"Huh?" Selena blinked at her friend.

Katy burst into laughter. "Are you on another

planet, or what?" she cried. "You can't get changed
for the cast party if you don't get out of the car."

"Sorry," Selena murmured, surprised to find
that they were already parked in front of her house
on Fear Street. "I was thinking about *Romeo and
Juliet*."

Katy rolled her eyes. "We just finished with
this play! Do you ever think of *anything* else?"

"Well, occasionally I think about guys," Selena
joked. She led the way up the crumbling sidewalk,
opened the front door, and switched on a light.
"I wish my mom didn't have to work nights this
month," she commented. "I really wanted her to see
the play."

"She'll be able to see you in the spring play,"
Katy said.

"*If* I get the part," Selena reminded her friend.
She straightened the runner in the hallway, then
started up the creaky steps.

Everything around me is falling apart, Selena
thought. She hated living in such a shabby house.
But she knew it was all her mother could afford.
Money was tight since Selena's father had died.

"There's no way anyone else could be Juliet,"
Katy insisted, following Selena into her bedroom.
"I mean, Alison is good, but she's not as good as
you. Even she says so."

"Alison is just being nice," Selena answered. She dumped her backpack on the pink-and-white bedspread.

"I'll help you learn your lines for the audition," Katy offered.

"Mmm-hmm," Selena replied absently. But she already knew she didn't want help—she liked to learn lines by herself. "Why don't *you* try out for one of the parts?" she suggested. "You don't always have to be a stagehand, you know."

Katy snorted. "What part could I get? I—I'm too big to get a decent role." Katy was about twenty pounds overweight—and very self-conscious about it.

"Stop putting yourself down." Selena tried to keep the annoyance out of her voice. "There are lots of parts in the play. Maybe you could be Juliet's nurse."

Katy didn't respond.

Selena dipped a tissue in a jar of cold cream and began removing her stage makeup.

"Selena?" Katy said after a moment. "When we were little, did you ever think you'd grow up to be so popular?"

"Of course not," Selena replied. "I thought I'd be fat and unpopular forever."

"Like me," Katy murmured.

Selena ignored her. "But once I got interested

in drama, I stopped thinking about being popular. I just wanted to be a good actress."

"It happened so fast," Katy said. "I mean, you took one drama class and that was it. You lost weight, you started going out with Danny . . . and you were the star of the very first play you did."

"Pure luck," Selena reminded her. "The girl who had the lead had to leave school."

"I know," Katy agreed. "But everyone knows you're the best actress at Shadyside High. You might be good enough for a professional career."

Katy sank back against the pile of pillows on Selena's bed. She sighed. "I hope you never get so popular you aren't my friend anymore."

"Hey—no way!" Selena cried. "When I win the Academy Award, I'll get up there and say, 'I want to thank my best friend, Katy Jensen, whose willingness to climb up on the catwalk made it all possible.'"

They both laughed.

Selena finished wiping her face, then opened the closet. She pulled out jeans and a green sweater.

"Are those jeans new?" Katy asked. "What are they? A size three?"

"They're a seven," Selena replied, laughing. "I'm not that skinny!"

"Compared to how you used to be, you are,"

Katy replied. "Compared to me, you are."

"You could lose weight too," Selena pointed out. "It's not like I'm a diet goddess or something."

"For sure," Katy scoffed.

"I'm serious," Selena insisted. "I lost weight because I wanted to do drama. I knew I couldn't get lead parts unless I stopped eating so much."

"That's the difference between you and me," Katy said. "I never cared about anything as much as you care about drama."

Selena glanced at her friend in exasperation. "Well, find something to care about," she said. She pulled her hair back and tied it with a green hair band. "How do I look?" she asked.

"Awesome," Katy replied. She glanced at her watch. "We'd better get going."

"We don't want to get there too early," Selena said. "We—"

She stopped when she heard the tapping at the bedroom window.

A soft tapping. Then louder.

A thump.

She spun around. Her eyes bulged with terror.

"Katy—" she choked out. "Someone's at the window! Someone's *watching* us!"

3

Selena caught the fear on Katy's face as they both turned to the window.

And heard a clattering crash.

"You're right!" Katy cried. "There's someone outside!"

Ignoring her pounding heart, Selena hurtled to the window. She peered out into solid blackness.

"What is it? Who is it?" Katy said in a voice just above a whisper.

"No one's there," Selena reported, staring down at the small patch of lawn at the side of the house. "I—I think I just panicked. I mean, we're on the second floor, right? How could anyone—"

"But what was that crash?" Katy demanded, arms crushed over her chest. She hadn't moved from the center of the room.

"It's really windy. Maybe the wind blew something over," Selena told her.

Selena shuddered. The thought of someone peering through her window while she changed was creepy. But it couldn't be true.

"There's no way anyone could see in," she reassured Katy. "We're too high up."

"I guess," Katy murmured, eyes still on the window.

"Let's just go to the party." Selena grabbed her bag and skipped down the wooden stairs. Katy followed close behind.

Selena pulled open the front door. The wind had picked up. It fluttered her blond curls as she locked the door.

"It *was* the wind," Katy cried. "Look!"

Selena glanced in the direction her friend was pointing. In the side yard, a long, metal ladder lay on the ground below Selena's bedroom window.

"It must have blown over," Katy said.

"But what was a ladder doing there in the first place?" Selena asked.

"Right under your window," Katy murmured.

Selena stared at the ladder in disbelief. Could someone truly have been watching her get dressed? She gazed up at her window and felt a chill run down her back.

"This is kind of creepy," Katy whispered. "First someone sends dead roses and that frightening card. Then . . ." She swallowed hard. "Do you think someone is following you? *Stalking* you?"

"Stalking me? Don't get crazy, Katy," she scolded.

She stared at the fallen ladder. It was very windy, and there were no people—or cars—on the street. If someone had been looking through her window, he would have fallen with the ladder. And she would have heard a car driving away.

"There's got to be some other explanation," Selena decided. "Maybe my mom was fixing something on the house and she forgot to put the ladder away."

"Maybe," Katy replied. "But I doubt it."

"Help me put it in the garage," Selena said. She leaned down and picked up one end of the ladder. Katy reached for the other end—then stopped.

"Oh wow!" she cried.

"What is it?"

Katy pointed. "On the bottom rung!"

Selena squinted at the ladder. And spotted a small orange circle on the bottom rung.

A sticker of the sun.

4

I still say it's some kind of joke," Selena declared as Katy drove toward North Hills.

Katy snorted. "Then it's a sick joke. I mean, dead flowers? And climbing a ladder to spy on you?"

"We don't know for sure that anyone was on that ladder," Selena reminded her.

"Well, what about those sun stickers?" Katy persisted. "What kind of a sick joke is that?"

Selena didn't answer. She stared out the car window at the large black trees along Old Mill Road.

She couldn't wait to get to Mr. Riordan's house. At the party she could stop thinking about stickers and flowers and ladders. She would concentrate on having fun.

But Katy refused to drop the subject. She seemed really frightened. "Maybe some psycho saw you in the play. Maybe you *are* being stalked!"

Selena stared out the window and didn't reply.

"I read an article about how crazy people stalk actors and rock stars," Katy continued, turning onto Park Drive. "They follow them everywhere, watch everything they do—"

Selena laughed. "Great theory, Katy. But I'm not famous."

"You're famous in Shadyside," Katy argued. "You're the star actress at the high school."

Selena shrugged. "It still doesn't make sense. Why would anyone be that interested in stalking a high school senior?"

"It could be someone at school," Katy replied earnestly. "Some guy who likes you or hates you or something."

Selena shrugged again.

"Stalkers aren't like normal people," Katy continued. "They can be really dangerous. Sometimes they kill the people they're stalking."

"This guy is only leaving me stickers!" Selena exclaimed. "Besides, if it is somebody at school, then it means I know him. It's probably someone who—*I know!*"

"Who?"

"Danny Morris," Selena suggested.

"Danny?" Katy scoffed. "Why would Danny stalk you?"

"He's not *stalking* me," Selena sighed, rolling her eyes. "He wants me to get back together with him."

"No way!" Katy exclaimed. "You broke up over a year ago."

"I know," Selena replied. "But he's always bothering me. It's like he just can't believe I don't want him back. I wish he would leave me alone."

"Well, I'd take him off your hands if I could get him to look at me!" Katy joked.

Selena frowned. "Why are you always putting yourself down?"

"You know it's true," Katy replied. "He'd never want someone like me. He likes sexy, skinny girls. Like you."

Selena shrugged and glanced at her watch. "The party should be going full blast by the time we get there," she commented.

"Yeah," Katy answered absently. "I heard . . ." Her voice trailed off.

"You heard what?"

Katy didn't answer. Selena saw her staring into the rearview mirror. Without warning, Katy made a sharp right turn.

"Katy?" Selena cried over the squealing tires. "What's wrong? Mr. Riordan's house is in the other direction!"

"I know!" her friend replied. "But someone's following us!"

"Huh?" Selena twisted in her seat and saw bright headlights in the back window.

Katy made another sharp right. The lights faded, then swung back into the car window.

"He—he's staying right on our tail!" Katy cried. "It must be your stalker, Selena! He's trying to push us off the road!"

5

Selena braced her hands against the dashboard as Katy swerved around another corner.

Their tires squealed. The car skidded onto the curb, then bounced back onto the street.

"Katy—look out!" Selena cried.

"He's still behind us!" Katy responded, her voice shaking. "He's practically riding our back bumper! What should we do?"

"Calm down," Selena instructed her. "It's just some joker. Stop talking about stalkers. Turn back to North Hills. He'll speed away as soon as we stop at the party."

"Are you crazy?" Katy cried, both hands squeezing the wheel. "If he follows us to Mr. Riordan's house—"

"He'll speed away," Selena repeated. "He

wouldn't dare follow us *into* the house. We'll be safe there."

"But—"

"Do you have a better idea?"

"No," Katy admitted. "You're right." She turned left at the next light and sped toward North Hills. Every time she switched lanes, the car behind them also switched. When she sped up or slowed down, the other car matched her speed, staying on their back bumper.

"As soon as we get to Mr. Riordan's, I'm calling the police," Katy declared.

At last they pulled into the big, circular driveway in front of Mr. Riordan's house. The other car squealed to a stop behind them.

"What now?" Katy cried. She set the parking brake and turned to gaze out the rear window. "I'm not getting out while he's there!"

"I—I don't know what we should do," Selena stammered. "Maybe you should honk—"

Katy squinted into the rearview mirror, her features tight with fear. Selena caught a flash of terror in her friend's eyes. "Oh no!" Katy choked out. "He's getting out of his car. He's walking toward us! We're trapped!"

6

anny!" Katy breathed.

"I don't believe him!" Selena growled. She threw open her door, jumped out, then whirled to confront Danny. "Why were you following us like that?" she demanded. "Why did you try to scare us?"

"Whoa," Danny said, grinning at her. His eyes flashed in the light from the headlights. "It was just a joke. I thought I'd give you a thrill."

"A joke?" Katy cried shrilly. "You nearly pushed us off the road!"

"Sorry." Danny's grin grew wider. "I guess I just like being close to Selena."

Selena sighed. *Danny is so immature,* she thought. *I don't care* how *cute he is.*

"Selena," Danny murmured, moving close, so close she could smell the peppermint on his breath. "I have something I want to tell you."

Selena jumped away, angry that he had gotten so close. "Then find me later!" she said curtly. Ignoring his hurt expression, Selena followed Katy up the walk.

Selena pulled open the front door. She was greeted by a roar of music, laughter, and loud talk. A garland of red and white balloons floated along the ceiling of Mr. Riordan's living room.

"Well, look who's here," Mr. Riordan called, stepping toward them. "It's our leading lady!"

"Thank you, thank you," Selena said, performing an exaggerated curtsy.

"There's pizza and soda by the fireplace," Mr. Riordan told them. "Get something to eat and come on back over. I have an important announcement."

"Pizza, yum! I'm starved," Selena declared.

"Me too," Katy agreed. "But I'm always hungry." As the girls elbowed their way to the refreshment table, Selena noted that most of the drama club was already there. She saw Alison chatting in a corner with Jake.

I've got to remember to ask Jake about the black flowers and the note, Selena reminded herself.

"Hey, who's the major babe?" Katy asked as Selena poured some ginger ale. Selena glanced to the front of the room. Next to Mr. Riordan stood a tall boy. Selena took in his long brown hair, intense dark eyes, and soft, serious mouth.

"I've never seen him before," she replied. He looked older than most of the other boys at the party. To her surprise, he suddenly gazed straight at her, almost as if he knew her.

"Attention!" Mr. Riordan called. "Come on over here, everyone."

Selena balanced her plate of pizza and chips, then carefully made her way to a chair near the front of the room.

"This is Eddy Martin," the drama coach announced, gesturing at the new guy. "He's a second-year drama student at Waynesbridge Junior College. As part of his studies, Eddy will be interning with us for the rest of the semester. He'll sit in on stagecraft classes and help put on the spring play."

"Weird," Katy whispered to Selena. "We never had an intern before."

Selena barely heard her. She couldn't keep her eyes off the new boy. He was glancing around the room, nodding and smiling at everyone. But Selena remembered the way his gaze had landed on her.

"There's something about that guy," Selena murmured. "I feel as if I've seen him before."

"If I'd seen *him* somewhere, I'd remember!" Katy joked. "I wonder if he's going to work with the stage crew."

Selena turned to her best friend and smiled. "Why don't you go find out?"

Katy grinned. She pushed herself out of the chair next to Selena and approached Eddy and Mr. Riordan. Selena watched as the three of them chatted for a moment, then Katy walked back to the refreshment table.

Selena considered doing the same thing when Eddy abruptly settled into the empty seat next to her.

"Hi," he said, giving Selena a dazzling smile. "I've been wanting to meet you. I'm Eddy."

"Welcome to Shadyside," she replied. "I'm Selena Goodrich."

"Everyone knows who you are," Eddy said. "I've seen you in all the drama productions this year. You're very talented."

"Th-thank you," Selena stammered, a little embarrassed.

"You're probably used to people complimenting your acting," Eddy continued. "You're a natural. I thought you were awesome when you took over Simone Perry's role two years ago. That was your first leading role, right?"

"Um, yeah," Selena answered. "How did you know about that?"

"I saw the play," Eddy explained.

"You're kidding!" Selena was astonished. Eddy had been watching her two whole years ago! And he remembered her performance. Selena stared at him. There *was* something so familiar about him. . . .

"I've seen a lot of your plays," Eddy continued. "I think it's great that you've managed to keep your grades up while doing so many shows. Not many kids could do that."

"Well, I have to get good grades if I want to go to college," Selena replied absently.

Her head was spinning. How did Eddy know about her schoolwork?

"You know a lot about me," she said, trying to keep it light.

Eddy gazed at her intently. "I know a lot about the whole drama department," he explained. "After all, I'm going to be interning with you."

For a moment, Selena didn't answer. There was something very strange about Eddy's interest in her. He hadn't taken his eyes off her since he sat down. Selena studied his face, but saw nothing but friendliness.

"When do you start interning?" she finally asked.

"I'm going to be here for the tryouts for *Romeo and Juliet*," he told her. He leaned closer to Selena. "I can't wait to see your Juliet," he murmured.

Selena couldn't think of a thing to say. Eddy continued to gaze at her, his dark eyes burning into hers.

"Eddy"—Mr. Riordan's voice broke into Selena's thoughts—"come over here. There is someone I want you to meet."

"Catch you later," Eddy said, giving Selena another heart-melting smile.

"Making friends with the new intern, hmm?" Selena glanced up as Katy plopped back down in the chair.

"Sort of," Selena replied, still feeling a little dazed. "He's really intense."

"And he's cute," Katy declared.

"Oh really? I didn't notice," Selena joked. Her gaze fell on Jake, sitting in the corner by himself. Selena stood up. "Be right back," she told Katy.

She strode across the room and dropped into the space next to Jake on the sofa. "Hi, buddy!" she said, bouncing a little on the cushion.

"Hey, Moon," Jake replied lifelessly.

"What's wrong?" Selena asked. "You look sort of down."

"So?" he snapped. "Is there a law that everyone

has to be cheerful every single minute?"

"No, of course not," Selena said, drawing back. Why was Jake so grouchy all of a sudden?

"By the way," she started slowly. "Did you leave a little present for me back at school?"

"Excuse me? A present?"

"Did you leave a lovely bouquet of black flowers in my locker?"

"Are you nuts?" Jake exploded. "What are you talking about?"

"Calm down! I was just asking," Selena replied. "Someone left me flowers, and I thought it might be you. You're always pulling dumb jokes."

"Well, I haven't felt like joking lately," Jake grumbled. "Besides, black flowers don't sound too funny."

Selena nodded. "There was also a card. It said tonight was my last performance."

Jake gaped at her. "That's a joke?" he cried. "That's totally sick."

"It's no big deal," Selena replied. "But then Katy and I think someone climbed a ladder outside my bedroom window. And watched us in my room."

Jake swallowed hard. "Maybe you should tell Mr. Riordan. Or call the police. You know. Show them the card."

Selena thought about it. "Maybe I *will* tell Mr.

Riordan." She stood up and crossed the room to the teacher, who—for once—was standing alone.

"What's up, Selena?" he asked. "You look so intense."

"Well, there's something I want to talk to you about," she explained. "I mean, it's probably nothing, but—"

Before Selena could continue, she heard a frantic banging at the front door, so loud it rose over the music and voices of the crowded room.

"Huh?" She gasped and turned to the front door—along with everyone else.

The door opened slowly.

A moan floated into the silent room from outside.

Then a familiar figure stumbled into the living room.

Selena gasped in shock.

Danny Morris.

His once-handsome face was caked with dark blood.

"Help me!" he moaned. "Selena!"

He staggered forward. He reached blood-soaked hands out to Selena.

Then, with a groan, he fell at her feet and lay there, unmoving.

7

Selena screamed. She gazed down at the crumpled form at her feet. Danny lay in a dark pool of blood.

Selena gasped for breath. Her mind whirled.

She stood frozen, too horrified to move. Too frightened to help him.

Danny stirred and raised his head. He groaned. "I'd rather die than live without you, Selena."

Selena gasped again. Her whole body trembled.

Was he serious? Had he hurt himself because of her?

"Danny—no!" she cried.

He sat up abruptly. Pulled a handkerchief from his pocket. Began wiping the blood off his face. He grinned up at her. "Who's the best actor in the room?"

"You—you . . . *moron!*" Selena shrieked.

Danny tossed back his head and laughed. "Come on, Selena! You didn't really think I would *die* for you, did you?"

Selena glared down at him. She knew everyone in the room was watching her. Everyone was laughing at her.

Danny shook his head. "Wow, Selena. You must be the biggest egomaniac on the planet!"

Her face burning, Selena spun away from him. She heard laughter. Kids whispering to each other.

Selena took a deep breath to calm herself. "Very mature, Danny." She kept her voice as cold as she could. "You win the Academy Award for Best Total Jerk."

"That was a dumb stunt, Danny," Mr. Riordan agreed, his voice stern. "You really did scare us."

Danny climbed to his feet. "I couldn't resist!" he said. "I just wanted to show everyone that I can act. Now we all know who should be Romeo!"

"*I* don't know if we want you to appear in the spring play at all!" Mr. Riordan said, shaking his head. "That kind of behavior—"

"It was a joke!" Danny protested.

"We're all laughing our heads off," the teacher replied sarcastically. "Let's start up the music again, okay?" He turned and headed over to the CD player.

Selena decided to get some fresh air. She crossed the room to the patio door.

"I can't believe you used to go out with that guy," said a deep voice in her ear.

Startled, Selena dropped her hand from the doorknob. She turned to see Eddy's handsome face. "How did you know about me and Danny?" she demanded.

"Oh, I must have heard it from one of the other kids," Eddy replied. He gazed at her, and Selena felt tongue-tied by the intensity of his dark eyes.

"Mr. Riordan is signaling me again," Eddy told her. "He wants me to meet everyone in the drama club!" His dark eyes flashed. "But I'll talk to you later, Selena."

Selena watched Eddy leave. *Weird,* she thought. *He's so intense, but I like him anyway. At least he's more mature than Danny.*

Danny. Selena frowned, thinking of his dumb stunt. She felt so embarrassed that she had fallen for it. Selena gazed around the room. Were kids still laughing at her?

Maybe I'll just go home, she thought.

She wandered over to the refreshment table. "Have you seen Katy?" she asked Alison.

"She was here a while ago," Alison replied. "I think she's in the kitchen with Mr. Riordan."

Selena started for the kitchen, but Alison stopped her.

"You were awesome in this play," Alison said, staring intently at Selena. "And I know you'll probably get the part of Juliet." She stopped and took a deep breath. "But I want you to know I'm trying out too," she finished in a rush.

"Well, of course," Selena said, surprised. She and Alison had always had a good-natured competition for parts, and Selena expected it to continue. "Why should the spring play be any different?"

Katy came through the kitchen into the living room. She approached the refreshment table and grabbed a handful of peanuts. "What's up?" she greeted Selena and Alison.

"I think I want to go home," Selena told her. "It's getting late and I'm starting to crash. I'm always so wiped after a performance."

"Okay. I guess I'm ready to leave too," Katy shrugged. "Just let me get my keys. I left them in my bag in the other room."

"I'll wait for you outside," Selena decided. She thanked Mr. Riordan for the party, then crossed to the front door. She stepped outside into the cold air.

Overhead, a million stars sparkled in the black night sky. Selena felt a chill. She had the weirdest feeling—as if the stars were all eyes, a million eyes staring down at her.

All Katy's stalker talk is making me paranoid! she told herself, shaking the feeling away.

She started down the path—but stopped as a shadow swept over her.

A large figure stepped out of the shadows to block her way.

"Where are you going?" Danny's husky voice demanded.

"Home!" Selena answered coldly. She was in no mood for Danny after the trick he had pulled.

"Fine," Danny said. "But you're going home with *me*."

"In your dreams," Selena snapped. "Why would I go anywhere with you? Don't you get it? I don't want to get back together!"

Danny grabbed her arm roughly. "Selena—" he pleaded.

Selena yanked her arm away. "Just leave me alone!" she cried.

"I only want to drive you home," Danny insisted, his voice rising.

"Hey, what's going on?" cried another voice. Selena glanced up to see Jake standing at the edge of the walk.

"Butt out!" Danny snarled. He grabbed for Selena again.

"Whoa!" Jake grabbed Danny's shirt and spun him around.

"What's your problem? Leave her alone!" Jake demanded.

"Mind your own business!" Danny growled.

"Selena is *my* friend!" Jake argued. "If she needs a ride, *I'll* take her home!"

Every guy I know has gone nuts! Selena decided.

Danny shoved Jake with all his strength.

Jake shot Selena a startled look as he stumbled back onto the brick walkway. And toppled over.

"Ohhh!" Selena uttered a low cry as Jake's head hit the pavement hard, with a dull *thunk*.

Jake sprawled on his back on the sidewalk.

He didn't move.

8

"Jake!" Selena cried.

"Get up!" Danny ordered, breathing hard as he stood over Jake's unmoving body. "Get up!"

Jake stirred. He moaned and slowly pulled himself to his feet.

Selena started toward him. But Jake launched himself at Danny's legs, pulling the bigger boy down.

As Selena watched in horror, the two boys rolled over and over, pounding each other frantically with their fists.

"Stop! Stop it!" she screamed.

A jagged cut already covered Jake's forehead. Danny's nose began to spurt blood.

Selena grabbed the back of Jake's shirt and yanked with both hands. Using all her strength, she managed to pull him away from Danny. Before the boys could begin again, she stepped between them.

"Get out of the way!" Jake warned, wiping blood from his forehead, his chest heaving.

"No!" Selena insisted. "Jake, what do you think you're doing?"

Jake's eyes had looked glazed, but now they snapped into focus. "I'm—I'm sorry," he muttered.

"You're sorry, okay," Danny snarled. "You're so sorry, you're pitiful!"

"Shut up! Just shut up!" Selena demanded. "You guys are both crazy! I'm going home with Katy. I don't need a ride from anyone! And even if I did, I wouldn't take it from either one of you!"

Danny stared at her for a long moment, struggling to catch his breath. Then he spun around and strode back to the house. He pushed past Katy, who had just appeared on the porch.

"What's up?" she asked, hurrying down to Selena and Jake. "Did Danny get a nosebleed?"

"He tripped," Jake muttered bitterly.

Katy stared at him for a moment. "Selena?" she asked.

"I'll tell you in the car." Selena sighed wearily.

Jake followed the girls to Katy's car. "I'm sorry, Moon," he repeated. "You know I can't stand Danny."

"That's no excuse."

"But he's such a jerk!" Jake insisted.

Selena sighed. "I know."

Katy unlocked the car doors and Selena slid into the passenger seat. Jake stood holding her door.

"Danny thinks he can always be the star. He thinks he'll be Romeo in the spring play," Jake said. "But he won't. I'd rather see him dead."

Selena gasped and gazed up at him. He looked so pale and angry in the cold moonlight. "You don't really mean that, Jake. Do you? *Do* you?"

He turned and walked away without answering.

A distant ringing awakened Selena at dawn the next morning. She glanced at her clock radio and saw that it was five a.m. It took her a moment longer to realize that the ringing came from her bedside phone.

She groggily reached for it. "Hello?" she mumbled.

"We were together last night," whispered a voice.

"Huh?" Selena choked out.

"I'm watching you," the voice whispered hoarsely. "I'm always watching you, Selena."

"Hey, wait—!" Selena cried.

"Soon we'll be together forever," the voice rasped.

Selena sat up straight. She was wide awake now.

She gripped the phone tightly in her hand. "Who is this?" she demanded angrily. "What are you trying to do? Who is this?"

She heard a click and the line went dead.

9

Selena approached the familiar stone steps of Shadyside High. She ran up the steps, taking them two at a time, and yanked open the front door. Inside, she collapsed against the wall, feeling safe for the first time that morning.

"Hi, Selena!" Katy called, coming down the front hall. "It's chilly out!"

"Yeah," Selena agreed, shivering.

"Hey!" Katy cried, drawing closer. "What's wrong?"

"Nothing really." Selena sighed. "It's just . . . I guess it's these practical jokes. I'm starting to feel nervous all the time! I—I heard from him again this morning."

"Oh wow!" Katy exclaimed, shaking her head. "You should call the police. You really should. If there's a stalker—"

"There isn't any stalker, Katy," Selena insisted. "I think it's Danny. You saw how crazy he got at the party."

Katy twisted her face, thinking about what Selena had said. Then she pointed. "Look. There's Danny. Waiting at your locker."

"Good!" Selena cried. She set her face in a hard expression. Then she rushed the rest of the way down the hall and found Danny squatting by her locker.

He had a scrap of paper in his hand, and was trying to work it through the slats in the locker door.

"More threats?" she demanded.

Danny straightened up, startled. "Selena, I didn't hear you come up."

"Get away from my locker!" she cried, losing control. "Get away from *me*!"

"All right already," Danny snapped. "Don't blow a fuse! I just wanted to leave you a note."

"Oh great!" Selena cried. "How about more dead flowers, too?"

The anger left Danny's face. "Huh?" he asked. "What are you talking about?"

"You know exactly what I'm talking about!" she yelled. "The notes and the gross flowers and the creepy phone calls!"

"You've lost it!" Danny exclaimed. "I've never left you a note before. I never did any of that other stuff, either! I just wanted to apologize for the fight last night."

"Yeah. For sure," Selena snarled. "Let me see it." She held out her hand.

"Forget it!" Danny growled, snatching his note away. "I've changed my mind. I'm not sorry!" He turned and stalked off.

Selena watched him go, struggling to make her heart stop pounding. Was the note in his hand really an apology? she wondered. Or was it another threat, signed with a sticker of the sun?

"What light through yonder window breaks? It is the east, and Juliet is . . . *the Moon!*" Jake recited dramatically. He threw himself into the seat next to Selena.

"Juliet is the sun," she corrected him. She swatted him with her copy of the *Romeo and Juliet* script.

Selena was glad for a chance to stop reading her lines for the audition. She had been sitting alone in the back row of the auditorium, waiting for try-outs to start. Now Jake and Katy sat on either side of her.

Jake had been clowning around. But now his

expression turned serious. "Have you heard from the stalker?" he asked. "Do you really think it's Danny?"

Selena frowned at Katy. "I see you've been telling Jake every little secret, every thought of mine."

Katy blushed. She started to sputter an apology.

"Hey, I'm a friend, right?" Jake broke in. "I have a right to know what's going on."

Selena didn't want Jake to know she suspected Danny. Jake and Danny had never liked each other. The last thing Jake needed was another reason to hate Danny. Especially after their fight.

"I don't know," Selena replied cautiously. "I mean, I think it has to be someone in drama. Who else could have put those flowers in my locker?"

"You should tell Mr. Riordan," Jake said.

"But he hasn't *done* anything," Selena protested. "Just written some notes. Besides, I need a drama scholarship. If I tell Mr. Riordan, he might not cast me in the play."

"Why would Danny do such dumb stuff?" Jake asked.

Selena shrugged. "He's used to getting his way. But not with me. I think he's really angry that I don't melt at his feet."

"Yeah, well, nothing Danny does would surprise me," Jake muttered. "But he'll get away with it, as usual"

Selena studied his face. The circles under his eyes were darker than ever. She didn't think she'd ever heard Jake sound so bitter. "Jake? Is anything wrong?"

"No!" he snapped. "I mean, we're talking about your problems, not mine," he added in a calmer voice. "Danny gives me a pain. But I think I understand where he's coming from."

"Are you serious?" Katy demanded.

"I just mean I know what it's like to really want something and not be able to have it."

The auditorium doors flew open. Mr. Riordan entered and strode to the front of the room. Selena saw Eddy behind him.

"I'm glad to see so many of you here," Mr. Riordan announced. "We'll begin by casting the major parts." He pulled a card from his pocket. "Alison Pearson and Selena Goodrich are both trying out for Juliet. Come on up to the stage. And for Romeo, we have Danny Morris and Jake Jacoby."

"Jake!" Selena turned to her friend. "I didn't know you were trying out for Romeo."

"Why not?" he replied, avoiding her eyes. "It's just one more thing that Danny and I both want." He stood quickly, still not looking at her, and marched up to the stage.

"What's his problem?" Selena asked Katy.

Katy rolled her eyes. "Your guess is as good as mine."

Selena picked up her script and climbed hesitantly to her feet.

"Hey, you're going to be great," Katy assured her.

"Thanks," Selena murmured. She started up the aisle, but found Danny blocking her way.

"Once I'm Romeo, we'll be spending a lot of time together," he said with a smirk.

"I'm glad Romeo dies in the end," Selena said nastily. She hurried up to the stage before he could say more.

As she passed the first row of seats, Eddy caught her eye and flashed her a thumbs-up. "Hey, Selena," he called. "Break a leg!"

"Thanks, Eddy." She felt a fluttering in her chest. Suddenly, she wished Eddy wouldn't be watching her audition.

"I want the Romeos and Juliets to practice their lines while I speak to the others," Mr. Riordan announced.

Selena crossed the stage toward the wardrobe area where she liked to work on her lines. She always sat on the same bench. Sometimes she thought it gave her luck.

To her surprise, someone was already sitting there. Alison was perched on Selena's bench, hunched over a copy of the script, her back propped against the heavy wooden wardrobe cabinet.

"Hey, Alison," Selena greeted her.

Alison finished reading a speech. Then she slowly raised her eyes to Selena. "I guess this is your place, right? I'll go work somewhere else."

"No problem," Selena replied. "I don't own the bench. Besides, I've already been over the lines so many times they're making me dizzy."

"Are you sure you don't want me to move?"

"Positive," Selena told her. "In fact, I think I'll go outside for some air." She pushed open the door that led from the wardrobe area to the hallway behind the stage.

"O, Romeo, Romeo," she murmured to herself. "Wherefore art thou Romeo? Deny thy father and refuse—"

She stopped when she heard the scream.

A shrill scream of terror. Behind her.

Followed by a frightening crash.

And then silence.

A heavy, frightening silence that made Selena gasp.

10

Selena froze, struggling to catch her breath. Then she forced herself to move. She pushed open the door and made her way back onto the stage.

She heard frightened cries, murmurs of shock. And saw a circle of kids near the back of the stage.

What were they staring at? Why were they so upset?

She pushed her way through the crowd. "What's going on? What's happening?" she demanded.

She saw Alison's sneakers first. In such a weird position. Toes to the floor. Then a few inches of Alison's legs.

And then the wardrobe cabinet.

The huge wooden cabinet. On its side.

On its side *on top of* Alison!

"Oh nooooo!" Selena wailed.

She could see Alison's hair spread over the stage.

Facedown. She's facedown, Selena realized. Her arms stretched out. The play script still gripped in one hand.

Not moving. Not moving. Not moving.

And the giant wardrobe on top of her. Crushing her body. Crushing her back.

Crushing her.

Alison not moving. Hands so pale and stiff.

Crushed beneath the wardrobe. Her hair spilling over the stage like blood.

As Selena stared down at the ugly scene, she felt her stomach lurch. *I'm going to be sick,* she realized.

She cupped a hand over her mouth. Staggered back.

Back through the alarmed voices, the muffled cries.

Struggling to keep control. Seeing Alison's crushed body even with her eyes shut.

Frightened, shrill voices all around.

"Is she dead?"

"How did it fall?"

"Pull it off her!"

"No! Don't move it!"

"I said *pull it off*! Are you crazy?"

"Someone call nine-one-one!" Selena opened her eyes to see Mr. Riordan bent over Alison's body. "Call nine-one-one!"

"I already called!" Danny shouted from the auditorium. "They're on the way!"

"Is she—? Is she—?" Judy Mason stammered from the circle of kids. Judy was Alison's best friend.

"I don't know," Mr. Riordan replied in a trembling voice. "She was crushed under the wardrobe. I can't tell if . . ." His voice trailed off.

Selena heard a low moan.

Alison!

She saw Alison—the wardrobe now lying beside her—try to raise her head.

"Don't try to move," Mr. Riordan was telling her tenderly. He knelt beside her. "Don't try to move. Help is on the way."

Selena sighed with relief. *Please let her be all right*, she prayed.

She heard running footsteps and turned to see Katy dashing up the steps to the stage. "What happened?" Katy demanded breathlessly. "I had to get something in my locker. When I came back—"

"It's Alison," Selena told her. "The wardrobe cabinet fell over on her."

"No way!" Katy cried. "How? It's so heavy—it couldn't just fall."

"Maybe it was too full," someone said.

"Or maybe someone pushed it," Jake said to Selena.

"That's stupid!" Katy exclaimed. "Why would anyone want to hurt Alison?"

"Maybe they didn't want to hurt Alison," Jake pointed out. "Isn't that the place where Selena usually sits?"

Selena stared at him, too shocked to answer.

The auditorium doors swung open. Police officers and medics burst in.

A few seconds later, the medics were gently lifting Alison onto a gurney. Selena was relieved to see that Alison was talking with them as they worked. She even smiled at something one of the medics said.

"What did she break?" Judy Mason was asking the medics. "Did she break any bones? Is she in danger?"

Judy followed the medics as they wheeled Alison out of the auditorium.

Selena dropped down onto the stage floor, feeling relieved. Feeling totally drained.

Wiping sweat off his forehead, Mr. Riordan announced that tryouts would be postponed until the next afternoon. Some kids began drifting out of the auditorium, talking quietly, but excitedly, about what had happened.

The police stayed for a while, searching around backstage to determine how the accident had occurred.

Selena remained too, curious and upset, wanting to know exactly what had happened. She couldn't get Jake's words out of her mind. Had the "accident" been planned for her?

"Looks like your cabinet was overloaded," she heard one of the police officers tell Mr. Riordan. "Don't let it get so full. Better check out the legs. The front leg on the right is weak."

"It was an accident . . . right?" Mr. Riordan asked him. "It fell over because of the weight?"

The officer nodded. "Looks that way to me," he replied.

"Thank you, Officer," Mr. Riordan said gratefully.

A few minutes later, the auditorium stood silent and empty. Selena pulled herself to her feet and made her way over to the tall, wooden cabinet. *Are the police right?* she asked herself. *Did the wardrobe fall because it was too full?*

Or did someone push it over on top of her?

No! She answered her own question. *No. No. No.*

No one in here could do such a thing.

No one.

She ran her fingers along the door of the wardrobe. Beneath the handle she felt something sticky.

Surprised, she pulled her hand back—and stared at an orange sticker of the sun.

11

The next day after school, Selena trudged home from the bus stop, her head buzzing with unhappy thoughts. Wind and rain swirled around her, making the normally dark Fear Street corner appear even gloomier.

What's wrong with me? she thought. I should be thrilled.

The audition had gone well. She had easily won the part of Juliet. With Alison out of the running, there wasn't even anyone else to try out.

But winning the role this way didn't make her happy. Alison was in the hospital—and Selena felt responsible.

The Sun had intended to hurt Selena, not Alison. Katy and Jake had tried to convince her the sticker on the wardrobe was only a coincidence.

But Selena knew better. Someone had expected

Selena to be crushed under that wardrobe cabinet.

Selena's front yard was a sea of mud and she slipped on the steps as she climbed to the front porch. As she unlocked the door, she wished again that her mom didn't have to work so much.

She switched on the lights and climbed upstairs, hearing her footsteps echo through the empty house. She changed into dry clothes and settled down against the soft pillows on her bed, ready to take turns studying geometry and reading her lines for the play.

Outside the wind howled, shaking the trees and rattling the windows. But Selena felt warm and cozy as she began *Romeo and Juliet*.

How camest thou hither, tell me, and wherefore?

The orchard walls are high and hard to climb. . . .

Selena shut her eyes to fix the words in her memory. She was about to go on to the next line when the phone on her night table jangled.

She set down the script and reached for the phone. "Hello?"

"Selena, it's me. Danny."

For a moment Selena sat silently. She could feel the blood throb at her temples. "Hi, Danny," she finally murmured.

"How are you?"

"I'm fine," Selena said impatiently. "What do you want?"

"Well . . . I—uh—don't know how to say this," he stammered. "But you and I haven't gotten along so well lately."

"No kidding."

"I wanted a chance to talk to you, that's all. I thought maybe we could grab a hamburger or something. Did you eat yet?"

"Are you crazy?" Selena cried. "I told you I don't want to go out with you!"

Danny didn't answer for a moment. Then he exploded. "Why not?" he demanded. "All I'm asking you to do is spend a couple of hours with me!"

"I'm just not interested!" Selena shouted back. "Don't you get it?"

"Yeah, I get it all right. I get that you're too stuck up now to even talk to me. I think you were nicer when you were fat!"

"Think whatever you want!" Selena told him angrily. "I don't want to go out with you. I don't want to see you at all. I don't appreciate your comment about my weight. And I'm sick of your dumb jokes, too!"

"Excuse me? What jokes?"

"Those stupid sun stickers you've been leaving all over the place. Did you actually push the wardrobe on Alison, too? Are you that totally sick?"

"I told you last time, I don't know what you're talking about," Danny insisted. "I would never hurt Alison. I don't even *have* any stickers."

"Yeah, right," Selena scoffed. "Whatever."

"What is your problem?" Danny demanded. "Even if you don't want to go out with me, why do you keep making these stupid accusations?"

"Well . . ." Selena's breath came in deep gasps. "Well . . . *someone* is trying to hurt me!" she blurted out. "Someone is driving me crazy!"

She slammed down the phone.

She didn't mean to say that. She didn't want to say that.

She didn't want to talk to Danny anymore.

She grabbed up the script again. But her body was shaking too hard to read it.

An unwelcome idea filled her head. *Maybe he's not pretending,* she thought. *Maybe Danny isn't The Sun.*

Selena didn't really believe Danny had pushed the wardrobe on top of Alison—even if he *had* thought Selena was sitting there. She had a hard time believing he would try to hurt her.

Maybe it was a stranger, as Katy had suggested. Some stranger who had become obsessed with her.

Selena forced herself to return to the script,

but she couldn't concentrate. *Forget Danny,* she told herself. *Just think of the play.* She began to read again:

> *My ears have yet not drunk a hundred words*
> *Of thy tongue's uttering, yet I know the sound:*
> *Art thou not Romeo—*

Again the phone interrupted her.

"Hello?" she yelled into the receiver.

"Selena?" asked a deep voice. A new voice.

"Who is this?" she demanded.

"It's Eddy. Eddy Martin. From drama."

Her heart began to pound again, but for a different reason. "Eddy!" she cried. "Hi. How are you?"

"Well, I'm fine," he replied. "I called to tell you how terrific you were in the tryouts today."

"Thanks," Selena answered. "I still feel kind of bad about it, though. I mean, Alison didn't even get to audition."

"True," Eddy agreed. "But the important thing is that she's going to be all right. I just talked to Mr. Riordan and he said she could be back at school next week if everything goes okay."

"Excellent!" Selena cried. "That's great news, Eddy."

"Besides, the show must go on," Eddy declared.

An awkward silence.

"I—I'm looking forward to rehearsals," Selena stammered.

"Most people would be really nervous," Eddy pointed out. "Juliet is a big part."

"That's what makes it so exciting," Selena explained. "The bigger the part, the more confident I feel on the stage."

"Wow!" Eddy exclaimed. "It's hard to believe you're the same person. You used to be so shy! You were always wearing baggy clothes and hiding behind those big glasses. And now you're about to take on such a challenging role, and you're not even scared!"

Selena's breath caught in her throat.

How did Eddy know how shy she had been?

How did Eddy know what she used to wear?

She took a deep breath. "Eddy," she asked softly, "how do you know what I wore two years ago?"

Silence.

Selena held her breath as she waited for him to answer.

"I must have seen an old yearbook or some-thing," he said finally. "I know a lot about you, Selena. You'd be surprised. Listen," he added before she could ask more, "are you busy Friday night?"

"As a matter of fact, no."

"Good. I've got two tickets to a sneak preview

screening near the college. It's a Chinese film. It's supposed to be very funny. Would you like to go?"

"I'd love to!"

"Great." Eddy hesitated. "There's just one thing. Don't say anything to anyone in drama—especially Riordan."

"Huh? Why not?" Selena asked.

"I don't think I'm supposed to be going out with the girls in the drama club," Eddy admitted. "Or in the high school."

"Why? You're not a teacher or anything."

"Well, no," Eddy replied. "But why ask for trouble?"

"Okay," Selena agreed. "No problem. I don't want to get you in trouble. I won't tell a soul. Not even my mother."

"Cool. I'll pick you up around seven."

Selena hung up the phone and stared at the wall until the flowers on the wallpaper blurred. She couldn't believe it. Eddy had asked her out!

She'd never felt this way about a boy before. He seemed so interested in her. He remembered everything he had ever heard about her. Selena hugged herself and fell back against the pillows. She couldn't wait for Friday!

A brilliant flash of lightning split the sky outside. Selena sat up, startled. The house shook as a clap of thunder roared overhead. The lights flickered briefly and rain pelted hard against the windows.

I'd better make sure all the windows are shut,
Selena thought.

She quickly checked her mother's bedroom,
then ran downstairs and peered into each of the
other rooms. The kitchen window was open a crack,
and the rain had already soaked one edge of the
table underneath it. Selena hurried to close the
window. As she yanked it down, she glanced out at
the storm. A flash of lightning lit up a small bundle
lying on the porch.

Selena frowned. Had her mom left something
outside?

She pulled open the door, darted out into the
pounding rain, and quickly retrieved the soaked
package.

Back in the kitchen she went, wiping rain off
her forehead with one hand.

The rain-soaked package fell apart, the brown
wrapping paper dissolving in her hands.

Selena breathed in a foul odor. Heavy and sour.

"Ohhhh." The odor sickened her.

And then—when she saw what she held—she
dropped it to the kitchen floor.

And retched.

And went running to the sink, gagging, cover-
ing her mouth, unable to hold down her disgust.

12

Rain pattered against the floor. Turning from the sink, Selena saw that she'd left the back door open.

The rat lay in a puddle of brown wrapping paper near the door.

The dead rat.

Already half-decayed. Its wiry legs stiff. Its patchy fur matted. Its head . . .

Its head chewed to a pulp. Chewed by a cat or some other animal.

A headless dead rat.

The disgusting aroma floated through the room, attacking Selena's nostrils again.

She held her breath. Fought back another wave of nausea.

And who had sent it? she wondered, feeling so frightened, so overwhelmed by the ugliness of it.

Who had such a sick mind? Who had left such a sick gift on her kitchen stoop?

She stumbled toward it. Spotted the orange circle on the soaked brown wrapping.

Recognized the sun. The sun. The sun—again.

And found the note, scrawled on the inside of the wrapper. The rain-smeared note in heavy black letters. Not too smeared to read:

> *Selena—*
> *This is you!*
> *This is you—unless you leave the*
> *play.*
> *I made a mistake yesterday. I crushed*
> *the wrong girl.*
> *But I'll get it right.*
> *If I can't be with you, no one else can,*
> *either.*
> *Don't be a rat, Selena. Because . . .*

The rest of the words were washed out by the rain.

Selena stared at the note, trying to steady her hand. She read it again. Again.

In the beginning, the note had seemed part of a joke. But no longer. *This has gone too far,* Selena thought numbly.

The Sun really wanted to hurt her. Whoever he was, he had made a mistake when he injured Alison instead of Selena.

There was no doubt about what the next part of the note meant. It was a clear threat. If Selena didn't quit the play, he'd kill her.

She'd be a dead rat.

Was he outside now? she wondered. Had he waited around to see her take in the package?

She hadn't heard a car drive up. But then how could she hear anything over the pounding of the rain?

Walking around the decayed rat, she peered out through the open door. The rain poured down, sheet after sheet. She saw only the rain, the darkness beyond it, broken by the bright flicker of jagged lightning.

Selena slammed the door and locked it.

A cold shudder ran down her body. She had to throw away the rat. She had to mop the floor. She had to rid the house of that sickening odor.

And then what? she wondered.

And then what do I do?

Back up in her room, she tried to concentrate on the script. But the picture of the headless, decayed rat lingered in her mind. Refused to fade away.

I'll call Katy, she decided. *I'll call Katy and tell her what happened. She always makes me feel better.*

Katy picked up the phone on the third ring. "Selena? What's wrong? You sound terrible!"

"Oh, Katy, I can't believe it!" Selena cried. She poured out the story of everything that had happened that evening. When she finished, Katy remained silent for a moment. Then she let out a long sigh.

"I said all along that someone crazy was after you," she scolded Selena. "But I'll do everything I can to help you find out who it is. We know it's someone in drama, right? So we'll keep an eye on everyone working on the play."

"Thanks," Selena breathed. "But he knows where I live. He knows—"

"Selena, do you think maybe you *should* quit?" Katy asked softly. She sounded very frightened. "If this nut is serious about his threat . . ."

"Quit the play?" Selena gasped. "I can't!"

"You don't have to give up acting forever," Katy suggested. "Just the spring play."

"But this play is the most important one! It's my only chance for a scholarship to Northwestern."

"Well, you *have* to tell Mr. Riordan what's going on," Katy insisted. "It's too serious not to tell him."

"What if he calls off the play?"

"Your life is more important than the play," Katy told her sharply.

"You're right." Selena sighed. "I'll tell him."

"Good. Don't forget. Tell him first thing tomorrow." She paused. "Are you okay? Want me to come over?"

"Thanks, but I'm okay," Selena replied. "I feel better just talking to you."

Katy sighed. "Well, the more you can keep your mind off this creep, the better. Which reminds me — have you thought about which videos we're renting for our sleepover on Friday?"

"Oh wow, Katy! I totally forgot we were doing that. I just made a date for Friday."

For a moment Katy didn't speak. "Couldn't you change it?" she asked.

"I don't think so," Selena replied. "Why don't we do the sleepover Saturday instead?"

"All right," Katy agreed. "It's not like I have any other plans. Who are you going out with?"

Selena knew she was supposed to keep it a secret. But she couldn't keep the news from her best friend. "You'll never believe it. Eddy."

"Eddy, the intern? But he goes to college. Isn't he a little old for you?"

"Not really," Selena replied. "I mean, he's only

two years older than me. And he's so sweet. I've only talked to him a few times, but I already feel as if I've known him my whole life. And I feel as if he knows me."

"Well, you know what you're doing," Katy said dryly. "I've got to get back to my homework."

"Okay," Selena replied. "Thanks for under-standing."

"No problem," Katy told her. "But, Selena, please be very careful. I really think you're in danger."

Katy's last words lingered in Selena's mind as she hung up the phone. *Even if it's true,* she decided, *I can't think about it all the time.*

She propped the script on her pillow and dropped onto her stomach, studying the lines again. She couldn't seem to memorize a single speech.

The rain drummed against her window. The wind howled, making the window rattle. Selena realized she couldn't concentrate because of the booming thunder.

Selena remembered the night she and Katy had found the ladder out in the yard. She sat up quickly and looked out the window.

No one there. *No one is looking in,* she told herself. But she stood up and closed the curtains, making sure they overlapped in the center.

The lights flickered, and again Selena set the script down with a sigh. There was no way she could memorize any lines till the storm stopped. But maybe she could at least get a start on her history paper.

She reached over to her desk and slipped her history book from the bottom of a pile of schoolwork.

A deafening thunderclap shook the house.

No one out there, she told herself. *Stop scaring yourself, Selena. Stop it right now.*

But what if the stalker had returned?

If he was out there, she realized, how could she know? If he broke into the house, how could she hear him over the storm?

Selena shut her eyes to force away her frightening thoughts. But in her imagination a silent, dark figure appeared. She watched him steal into the house, creep up the stairs, approach her door.

Selena's eyes flew open.

Another bolt of lightning sent long shadows across her room.

Stop it! she scolded herself again. *You're letting your imagination run away with you. It's just a stupid rainstorm.* She shut her eyes again.

Maybe I should just forget homework and go to bed early, she thought.

She settled back on the bed, trying to relax. The world outside flickered on and off as lightning crashed and rain thundered against the trees of the Fear Street Woods behind her house.

And then she heard something over the noise of the storm.

The thud of heavy footsteps.

Footsteps in her house.

Selena's breath caught in her throat. She sat up in bed, her heart hammering in terror.

Had she forgotten to lock the back door? Had someone broken in through one of the windows?

She sat silently, her breathing shallow, trying not to hear the rhythmic sounds.

Thump ... thump ... scrape.

The footsteps came closer. Someone was on the stairway.

Someone was in the house.

The Sun?

Scrape ... scrape ... thump.

Closer. He was almost at the top of the stairs now.

Moving silently, Selena slid off her bed. She unplugged her metal reading lamp. She grasped it by the base, felt its comforting weight in her hand.

Then she stepped behind the door and waited.

13

Selena hunched behind the door, waiting . . . waiting for the stalker.

Holding her breath, she gripped the lamp.

A flash of lightning lit up the hall. In the white glow, Selena saw a shadow.

She drew in a sharp breath. The stalker had reached the top of the stairs. She heard his footsteps over the hall carpet.

"Selena?"

Selena raised the lamp higher.

"Are you up here, honey?"

Selena felt a rush of relief so strong she almost dropped the lamp.

"Mom!" she sobbed. "You're home!"

She tossed down the lamp, plunged into the hall, and hugged her mother.

"I'm so glad you called my name!" Selena cried.

"I was getting ready to nail you with my lamp."

Her mother laughed. "Sorry I scared you. I know how you hate to be by yourself in a storm. The lightning knocked out the electricity in town, so the restaurant had to close. Which means I get to see my daughter for a change!"

"Well, I'm glad you're here," Selena said again.

"I have an idea," her mother said, smiling. "Let's light a big fire in the fireplace, and I'll make a pot of hot chocolate."

"Great!" Selena agreed.

While her mother built the fire, Selena prepared the hot cocoa in the kitchen. Then she settled on the sofa next to her mom.

She loved looking at her mother in the firelight. She thought her mother was beautiful. Selena had inherited the same pale blond hair and green eyes.

As they sipped the hot chocolate, Selena told her mother about the spring play.

"You'll be a wonderful Juliet," her mother gushed. "Even if I have to call in sick to work, I'm going to see you in this one."

"Great," Selena replied. "I just wish Dad could see it too."

"So do I, honey," Mrs. Goodrich said softly. "He'd be so proud of you."

Selena nodded sadly. Her dad hadn't lived to

see Selena on stage, had never known about her acting talent. "I miss him so much," Selena told her mother. "It's been three years, but I still keep expecting him to come home as if nothing had happened."

"I know," her mother replied, glancing away. "But you know, honey, he'll always be with us, both of us, as long as we remember him."

They sat in silence for a moment, then Mrs. Goodrich turned to Selena, forcing a smile to her face. "Tell me more about school," she urged. "I want to know everything that's going on."

Selena couldn't help thinking about the stalker, the dead rat, the ugly threats. Should she tell her mother?

"I've got a couple of term papers due," she said. "But other than that, there's not much happening, except . . ."

"What?"

"Nothing." Selena shrugged.

I'll tell Mr. Riordan instead, she thought. *There's no sense worrying Mom. She's got enough to handle.*

"I'm a little stressed," she told her mother with a smile. "But believe me—the play is the only thing I care about."

● ● ●

The next morning, Selena was hurrying from math class to English when she bumped into Jake, nearly knocking him over. "Whoa!" she cried. "Sorry, Jake! I didn't see you."

"Hey, Moon," Jake muttered lifelessly.

"Is something wrong?" she demanded.

He frowned. "Mr. Riordan just posted the cast list for the spring play."

"Really?" Selena cried. She stepped up to the bulletin board to see.

"No surprises," Jake told her. "You're Juliet, naturally. And Danny is Romeo."

"Yuck!" Selena wrinkled her nose. "I was hoping you would get it."

"I *should* have gotten it!" Jake exclaimed with surprising heat. "You saw the auditions! I was a thousand times better than that jerk."

"You were both good," Selena said carefully.

"Danny only got it because he's always kissing up to Mr. Riordan," Jake raged. "I thought maybe *once* talent would make a difference. But Danny always gets his way." He kicked a balled-up piece of paper across the hall.

"I'm really sorry you didn't get the part," Selena told him honestly. "But I'm surprised you even tried out for it. I mean, until now, you only wanted character parts."

"Is that what you thought?" Jake cried shrilly. He glared at her. She took a step back, startled by his anger.

"Did you really think I was happy to take character parts while you were the star?" he demanded.

"Well, I—I just assumed—" Selena stammered, not knowing what to say.

Jake scowled. "We've been friends for a long time, Selena, but there's still a lot about me you don't know."

"Jake, I'm sorry—"

"Forget it!" Jake shook his head. He turned away from her. "I'll tell you one thing. Danny isn't going to get everything he wants. Not this time!"

"Jake, stop saying things like that," Selena pleaded. "You're scaring me. You really are."

He didn't seem to hear her. He had turned and was already halfway down the hall, his hands clenched into tight, angry fists.

"I'm psyched about working on the play," Katy said as she and Selena waited for the bus. "I can't wait for rehearsal tonight."

"Me neither, except . . ." Selena's voice trailed off.

"Except what?" Katy demanded. "Are you thinking of dropping out of the play?"

"No. No way," Selena told her. "But I'm definitely going to say something to Mr. Riordan—and who knows what he'll do."

"We'll just have to wait and see," Katy said.

Selena changed the subject. "I'm really worried about Jake. I don't know why he's so messed up. But he's been acting as if I'm his enemy instead of one of his oldest friends."

"You mean you don't know?" Katy asked incredulously.

"Huh? Don't know what?" Selena demanded.

"Selena." Katy sighed. "I thought for sure Jake had said something to you. I can't believe he didn't."

"Didn't say something about what?" Selena shrieked. "Will you stop keeping me in suspense?"

"Well, I found out yesterday why he's been so weird and moody all the time. It's because of his parents. They're splitting up."

"Oh no!" Selena gasped. "Mr. and Mrs. Jacoby? I can't believe it!"

"I guess it's been pretty tough on Jake," Katy continued. "To tell you the truth, I'm really worried about him too. He's just been so unpredictable lately. It's like you never know what he's going to do next. And he's letting everything get to him."

"Well, that's true," Selena agreed. "Like this thing with Danny. I know they never liked each other, but it's really getting out of control."

Katy nodded. She stepped out into the street, searching for the bus. No sign of it.

She sighed. "So you're really going to tell Mr. Riordan about the stalker?" she asked, her expression turning serious.

Selena nodded. "I guess." Deep down, she still wasn't sure she wanted to tell the drama coach what had been happening.

He'll have to cancel the play, she thought. *And if the play is cancelled, I won't get a scholarship. And that's the end of all my big plans.*

"Don't say you guess. You should tell him right away," Katy scolded. "I mean, who knows what that creep is planning next?"

Selena heaved a big sigh. *What a bad-news time,* she thought. Jake's parents were splitting up. Danny was playing Romeo. And she was being stalked.

The only bright spot in her life right now was her date with Eddy on Friday night.

"We've been waiting for you," Danny called from halfway up a tall ladder. "O, Juliet, Juliet—wherefore art thou Juliet?" he boomed.

Kids laughed.

Selena rolled her eyes. "Give it up," she

snapped. This was not the way she wanted to start the first rehearsal. She climbed onto the stage, trying to ignore Danny.

He dropped from the ladder and landed in front of her. "Listen, we have to work together until the play is over. Can't you at least *try* to get along with me?"

"You're right," Selena admitted. "I'm just a little on edge." She took a deep breath. "And I'm really scared of the balcony scene," she added, glancing up at the ladders being used to build the set.

"Oh right." Danny laughed. "I forgot. Juliet is afraid of heights!"

"Maybe we should make it a *basement* scene!" someone suggested from out in the auditorium.

More laughter.

Selena ignored it. She pulled her script from her pack and joined the others at centerstage.

"Where's Jake?" Mr. Riordan called. "We need him for the first scene."

"Jake?" someone called. "Hey—Jake!"

Jake shuffled onto the stage, a scowl creasing his face. "Hey, what's the big deal?" he muttered.

"Come on, everyone," Mr. Riordan insisted. "Let's get down to business. Now, Act One, Scene One. Let's just read through it."

Concentrate. Concentrate, Selena ordered

herself. On cue, she began speaking her lines, and within a few moments she was into her part. Without even trying, she felt herself relax. Selena was surprised at how well the first rehearsal went. Once they got started, everyone was into it, even Jake.

As she said her lines, moving about the stage, a part of her stayed aware of Eddy, seated next to Mr. Riordan in the front row.

Was she just imagining his eyes on her, following her every move? Was he watching the others as intensely?

During a scene break, she glanced down at him and saw him respond with a smile, obviously meant for her.

As she read her lines for the next scene, she almost felt as if she were speaking them directly to him.

"Okay, people, it's going well," Mr. Riordan announced after about an hour. "Now I'd like to try something a little different. Juliet, I want you to stand upstage and say your lines more quietly. I also want Juliet's father—Jake? Where did Jake go?"

"Sorry," Jake called. "I went backstage for some water."

"Next time, wait for a break," Mr. Riordan snapped. "Anyway, I want you to stand over there."

He pointed toward the rear of the stage. "When she starts to speak, move upstage. Get it?"

"Of course I get it," Jake grumbled. "How hard is that?"

Mr. Riordan sighed. "Is everyone ready?" he asked.

Selena stepped to where Mr. Riordan had indicated and began to read her lines.

"Again," the teacher called. "Try to get more feeling into it, while your father looks on."

Selena repeated the lines. She loved this part of rehearsal. She loved the sense that she was a part of something that was always changing, always developing.

"Excellent!" Mr. Riordan called.

"That was great!" Eddy echoed.

"Let's try to get the same feeling in the next scene," Mr. Riordan instructed. "Juliet, I want you to—"

His voice was cut off by a shrill scream.

"The lights! The lights!"

Selena recognized Katy's voice. Gasped as Katy dove into her.

The pages of her script flew out of her hand.

Katy tackled her to the floor.

Selena didn't even see the bank of spotlights fall.

But she heard the crash. Felt the stage rock. Heard the shatter of glass. The crunch of metal.

Heard the high screams of horror all around.

And knew that she was dead.

14

I'm dead, Selena realized.

Katy and I . . . we're both dead.

Crushed under the big metal lights.

Again she heard the crash. The crunch of metal. The splintering of glass.

And waited for the pain.

But she felt no pain. No pain at all.

Because I'm dead, she knew.

I'm dead now, floating in silence.

She opened her eyes to see the horrified faces of her friends. Mr. Riordan leaned over her. Shouting. What was he shouting?

She saw Eddy, too. His face so pale. His eyes so wild.

With grief?

The sounds of their cries finally reached her ears.

She swallowed. She breathed.

Not dead.

She tried to raise herself. No pain—except for a throbbing in her right knee.

No pain.

I'm alive. I'm okay. The lights fell to the stage— and missed me. Missed me because Katy . . .

Katy?!

Selena raised herself to her knees. Saw Katy lying on her stomach. At such a strange angle. Her body twisted. Her arm . . . ?

Her arm caught under a shattered spotlight?

She saw Eddy, on his knees beside Katy. "Stay still," he was warning her. "Don't try to move. Your arm . . ."

Was it crushed? Was it bleeding? Selena, dazed, pulled herself to her feet.

"I think it's just bruised," Katy said, groaning.

Katy is okay too, Selena thought.

She watched Eddy gently examine Katy's injured arm. "Can you move it?" he asked.

"It—it's okay," Katy stammered. An angry red bruise had started to form an inch below the elbow.

Mr. Riordan helped Katy to her feet. "It's not broken," he said. "But you're going to have a bad bruise. Jake, go get some ice from the cooler in the back."

As Jake took off, Mr. Riordan and Eddy turned to the four spotlights, connected by steel rods. "We check those lights every month," Mr.

Riordan said, scratching his head. "How could they fall like that? How?"

I know how, Selena thought grimly.

The stalker. The same person who pushed over the wardrobe cabinet. He did it. He sent the lights crashing down.

He tried again to kill me. And Katy saved my life.

And got hurt. The second person to get hurt because of me.

Getting a scholarship isn't worth putting my friends in danger, Selena decided. *I've got to put a stop to this. Now.*

She turned to Mr. Riordan. "Can I talk to you for a moment?" she asked in a trembling voice.

His face tightened in surprise. "Well, I have to make sure that Katy—" he started.

"I have to tell you something," Selena insisted. "Something really frightening."

"Oh. Okay." The teacher followed Selena to the back of the stage.

As Selena led the way, trying to decide where to begin her story, she glanced back. And saw Eddy staring at her.

A cold, thoughtful expression on his face that startled her.

Why is he watching me? Selena wondered. *Why is he staring at me like that?*

15

Dear Selena,
Today we were together again.
Something bad happened. Something
very bad.
I made it happen, Selena.
You don't realize it, but we are
together more and more every single
day. Even when you don't see me, we
are together.
I have you in my power, and you don't
even know it. But you will know
soon, Selena.
If you perform in Romeo and Juliet,
you will know the truth. And it's the
last thing you'll ever know.
The Sun

16

"xcellent movie!" Eddy said as he and Selena strolled through the theater parking lot.

"That actress was awesome," Selena agreed. "I didn't even read the subtitles. I just stared at her face."

"That will be you someday," Eddy teased.

"Oh really? You think I'll need subtitles?" Selena cracked. Eddy opened the car door for her. She settled into the bucket seat of the red Honda Civic and shut her eyes for a moment. The car reminded her of Eddy—warm and comfortable.

When he first picked her up, Selena had felt uncertain and awkward. But the more time they spent together, the more relaxed she felt.

"Where next?" Eddy asked, climbing in beside her. "Are you hungry?"

"I shouldn't be, after all that popcorn," Selena

admitted. "But actually, I'm starved."

"Me too," Eddy agreed. "Ever been to Sam's?"

"Sam's? No," Selena replied. "Where is it?"

"It's a great burger place in Waynesbridge near the junior college," Eddy told her. "Want to try it?"

"Sure," Selena said. Actually, she thought that if Eddy had suggested going to a place that served baked worms, she'd probably agree to it!

"Do you like jazz?" Eddy asked, slipping a cassette into his tape deck.

"I don't know much about it," she replied.

"My dad got me hooked on it," Eddy told her. "At first I didn't like it. But now it's my favorite, even more than rock music. This is an old tape. By Bill Evans. He was a great piano player."

Selena listened to the music as they drove along the dark highway to Waynesbridge. "It's kind of nice," she told Eddy.

"You might like something newer," he told her. "I have a great new Wynton Marsalis tape. We can listen to it on the way home."

He guided the car through a narrow tunnel, then pulled into a space in an underground parking lot.

Eddy led Selena back through the tunnel and up a flight of concrete stairs. Pushing open the door at the top, Selena stepped out into an area of small restaurants and shops. The walks were paved with cobblestones.

"This is cool!" she declared.

He smiled. "Yeah, it's part of the campus. The college drama majors hang out at Sam's a lot. The owner used to be an actor in New York. People bring their parents here because the shops are so nice."

"I love it!" Selena gushed. "I'll bet it has a really different crowd than the places I usually go."

Eddy pulled open the front door of Sam's, and the greasy aroma of burgers and fries drifted out. A waitress led them to a dark wood booth in the back. Selena settled in, glancing around at the sports posters on the walls.

"The food here is not too shabby," Eddy told her. Their waitress arrived and they each ordered a burger and fries, with root beer for Selena and a Coke for Eddy.

"So how are you doing on your lines for the play?" Eddy asked.

"I've memorized all of acts one and two," Selena reported.

"The scenes I've seen you do were excellent," Eddy praised her. "You hardly need any direction. You have a lot of talent, Selena."

"Thanks," she murmured, embarrassed. "But I keep thinking I haven't gotten the character right.

There are some things I don't understand about Juliet."

"That's why you're so good," Eddy said intently. "Most high school performers just say the lines. You really think about it and try to do your best."

"But what if my best isn't good enough?" Selena demanded, fiddling with the metal napkin holder. "I mean, the drama coach from Northwestern will be coming to opening night. My only chance of going to college depends on how I do."

"You'll definitely get the scholarship," Eddy replied. "But if you're worried about it, I can coach you."

"Are you serious?" Selena cried.

"Sure," he said, flashing her a dazzling smile. "I'd be happy to. But don't tell anyone else."

"I won't," she promised. "Are you sure it's okay?"

"Definitely," Eddy replied. "I just don't want Mr. Riordan to think I'm playing favorites."

"I understand," Selena assured him. She smiled at the thought of having a secret romance with Eddy. He made her feel so comfortable, so close to him.

"You know," Eddy continued, "you *are* my favorite, Selena. And I want to get to know you better. I don't usually meet people who love performing as much as you do. And I think it's amazing that you've stuck to it. I know you've been through a lot in the past few years. It must be tough for you without your father, but you haven't let that stop you."

Selena's mouth dropped open. "How do you know about my father?" she asked. "I never told you he died."

"Mr. Riordan told me," Eddy said. "I'm sorry. I guess I shouldn't have mentioned it." He reached across the table and took her hand. "I really care about you, Selena."

Selena gazed back at him, suddenly uncomfortable.

"I realize you're very busy," Eddy went on. "And I've seen how popular you are. But I'd like to be with you . . . I mean, whenever you have time."

Selena didn't know what to think. She found Eddy so attractive—but what did she really know about him?

Nothing.

And yet he seemed to know so much about her.

So much that she had never told him.

She pulled her hand back. "I'd like to see you too, Eddy," she said. "But—"

"But what?" Eddy interrupted. "Do you already have a boyfriend?"

Confused, Selena shook her head.

"Do you think I'm too old for you? Is that it?" He gazed at her earnestly.

What's going on? Selena asked herself. *I really like Eddy! Why am I so suspicious?*

"I'm sorry," Eddy said. "I guess I've been coming on too strong."

"It's not that," Selena replied. She felt torn. On the one hand, she liked Eddy and wanted to confide in him. On the other hand, she felt afraid to trust him. Afraid to trust anyone.

"What's wrong, Selena?" he asked gently.

"It's—it's—Someone has been threatening me," she blurted out.

"Excuse me?"

"I know it sounds crazy," Selena cried. "But someone has been leaving me ugly notes and horrible, frightening presents. I don't know who I can trust anymore!"

"Wow," Eddy murmured. "Do you have any idea who it is?"

"Not really," Selena replied hopelessly. "But I think it's someone in the drama club."

"Oh wow," Eddy repeated, shaking his head. "I feel so bad for you."

Haltingly at first, and then more quickly, Selena found herself telling Eddy everything that had happened, from the first bouquet of black flowers through the most recent note.

"And the most frightening part is that . . . that I think this guy pushed the wardrobe over on Alison and dropped the lights on Katy. Trying to get me."

"It's possible," Eddy agreed. "But it's so unbelievable! I mean, would someone we know actually try to *kill* you?"

Selena sighed. "Katy thinks it's a stalker. Like those crazy people who get obsessed with movie stars. But I'm not even famous."

"You're pretty well known in Shadyside, though," Eddy said thoughtfully. "Did you tell Mr. Riordan?"

She nodded. "He thinks the wardrobe and the lights were accidents. He thinks the notes and horrible gifts were someone playing a sick joke. He said he'll be more alert than ever. But he doesn't think I'm in any real danger."

"Maybe you should go to the police," Eddy said, lowering his voice.

"They'd probably have the same reaction as Mr. Riordan," Selena protested. "Accidents and dumb jokes."

Eddy sighed. "I'll think about this," he said. "Maybe there's some way I can help you feel safer."

"Thanks, Eddy," Selena replied. "I appreciate it."

He picked up the check and flashed her a thumbs-up. "Back in a minute," he said.

Selena watched him walk to the cashier. *I'm glad I told him everything,* she thought. *He really understands.* She glanced past Eddy, to the front of the restaurant.

Danny Morris stood in the doorway.

Staring hard at her.

Selena caught her breath.

What is he doing here? she wondered, feeling anger—and fear.

Did he follow me?

What does he want?

*S*elena felt all her muscles tighten.

This place is not a high-school hangout, she thought. *It's miles from Shadyside.*

There could be only one explanation. Danny followed her! Trembling with fury, Selena leaped up from the booth and stepped into the aisle, blocking Danny's path.

"Hey—Selena!" he cried, pretending to be surprised.

"What are you doing here?" she demanded furiously. "Did you come to bother me some more?"

Danny didn't reply. He stared at her, his face filled with scorn. His lips curled into a sneer. "You really think you're the center of the universe, don't you, Selena?"

"Huh? Give me a break, Danny!" she raged. "I want to know why you followed me here."

He shook his head. "I brought my date here," he said finally. "She lives in Waynesbridge."

He turned to the door. A short, pretty girl with brown curls and big, brown eyes entered.

"Selena," Danny said, smirking, "this is Susie. Susie, this is Selena. She goes to Shadyside with me."

"Uh, hi, Susie," Selena choked out. Her face was burning with embarrassment. She wished the floor would open up and swallow her. "I've, uh, got to go," she mumbled. Then she turned and ran out the door.

Eddy waited outside.

"That was close!" He laughed.

Selena stared at him, confused.

"Danny," Eddy explained. "If he saw us together, he'd tell Riordan for sure."

"Oh right," Selena murmured. Eddy opened the door to the concrete stairway. Selena barely even noticed where they were going. She couldn't get Danny out of her mind.

He had another girlfriend. Or at least he was interested in another girl.

So he wasn't the stalker.

Not Danny, she thought. *Not Danny. Not Danny.*

Then who?

She followed Eddy down the steps to the tunnel.

There were no sidewalks, so Selena walked as close to the concrete wall as possible. Eddy stayed right beside her. "I have to tell you, Selena. I've waited a long time for this date," Eddy said.

"What do you mean?" Selena asked.

"Well—I was an upperclassman at Shadyside High when you first started in drama. I've really had my eye on you since then."

Selena walked along in silence. She couldn't believe it. Eddy had had a crush on her all this time!

"The only bad thing about this place is getting to the parking lot," Eddy commented, changing the subject. "But the food is worth it." He took her hand and gave it a squeeze. "Having a good time so far?" he asked.

"Definitely!" Selena replied. *The best time in ages*, she thought. *I finally feel safe.*

They were halfway through the tunnel when Selena heard a loud screech. It took her a moment to place the sound.

The squealing tires of a speeding car.

Selena spun around. A dark car with its lights out.

Roaring toward her.

She tried to dodge out of its way.

But Eddy grabbed her by both shoulders—and shoved her into the path of the hurtling car.

18

Selena's shriek of horror echoed off the concrete walls of the tunnel.

She felt herself staggering forward. Stumbling. Unable to stop.

She braced for the impact.

"Ohh!"

Her body smashed into something hard.

I've been hit!

But no. She had hit the wall. She felt a rush of air as the car skidded past her, its tires squealing.

"Selena! Are you okay?"

Selena didn't recognize the voice. Then, dazed, she turned to see Eddy beside her.

"What happened?" she gasped, pushing herself off the tunnel wall.

"The car—it almost hit us!" Eddy cried in a trembling voice.

"You . . . you pushed me in front of the car!" Selena accused.

"I pushed hard enough to be sure you'd reach the other side of the tunnel," he explained, struggling to catch his breath. "Then I jumped."

He let out a deep sigh. "Sorry it was a little rough."

Selena glanced around the concrete tube and shuddered. There was barely enough room for a car to squeeze by. If Eddy hadn't pushed her out of the way . . .

She wrapped her arms around her chest. She was beginning to tremble in reaction. "Don't apologize," she murmured. "You saved my life."

"Are you sure you're okay?" Eddy leaned close.

"Uh-huh," Selena said. "You?"

"I banged my elbow," he replied. "No big deal. I wish I'd been able to get that idiot's license number."

He offered Selena his hand and led her toward the parking lot. "We should have been walking on this side in the first place," he said, shaking his head.

Selena stared at Eddy in surprise. He had been here many times before. He must have known there wasn't enough room to walk in the tunnel.

We should have been walking on this side, Selena silently agreed.

Why, she wondered, *weren't we?*

• • •

"Did you see the license plate?" Selena asked as Eddy turned onto Old Mill Road. They'd been riding in silence for several minutes. Selena still felt jittery.

"No," Eddy admitted. "It happened too fast. It was obviously some jerk who'd had too much to drink. I hope the police get him before he kills someone."

"What if it wasn't a drunk driver?" Selena suggested. "What if it was someone who knew us? Who wanted to hurt us?" She swallowed hard. "Or wanted to hurt *me*?"

Eddy stayed silent for a moment. "You mean the guy who sent you the notes?" he asked quietly.

Selena nodded, staring straight ahead.

"But it happened over in Waynesbridge," Eddy pointed out. "No one would expect you to be there."

"Unless they followed me," Selena muttered, remembering her encounter with Danny.

Maybe that driver wasn't aiming for us deliberately, Selena thought, changing her mind. *Maybe Eddy just decided to push me in front of that car.*

She leaned her head against the car window and shut her eyes. *I can't trust anyone,* Selena thought.

When she opened her eyes and gazed at Eddy, she suddenly didn't feel so safe anymore.

The next morning, Selena awakened with the vague memory of a disturbing dream. She shook the feeling away, dressed quickly, and hurried downstairs.

She sliced bananas into two bowls of cereal. Today was her mother's day off. For once, the two of them could have breakfast together.

After setting the table and pouring orange juice, Selena stepped out onto the porch for the newspaper.

She gasped when she saw the cone-shaped package leaning against the screen door. Wrapped in blue tissue paper. Another bouquet.

"Oh no!" she wailed. "Not again!" She reached for the package, ready to toss it into the garbage can.

But then she saw something bright peeking out from the edge of the paper. Something bright and colorful—a beautiful red rose.

Selena brought the bouquet indoors and quickly unwrapped it. It was so beautiful—a dozen red roses nestled in green leaves. She couldn't find a card. But Selena didn't need one.

It's from Eddy, she thought. *It must be. How could I have suspected him? How could I think he wanted to hurt me?*

She stood on the kitchen stool and pulled a glass vase down from the shelf above the refrigerator. She filled the vase with water, then began to arrange the flowers and greenery.

"So beautiful," she breathed. She pressed her face into the blooms, inhaling their sweet scent. "Thank you, Eddy," she murmured happily.

"Good morning, honey," her mother called out behind her.

"Hi, Mom." Selena glanced up. "Look what someone left for me."

"How lovely," Mrs. Goodrich exclaimed, approaching the table.

"Smell them," Selena urged, once again burying her face in the bouquet. "They're wonderful!"

"Oh—wait!" Mrs. Goodrich suddenly cried. "Selena!" she gasped. "Get away from them!"

"Huh?" Selena had her face buried in the bouquet. She pulled it away. "What's wrong, Mom?"

"Those leaves, Selena—they're poison ivy!"

19

Selena had always been very allergic to poison ivy.

A few minutes later, her face had swelled up. Her skin tingled and itched. She found it hard to breathe. Her temperature rose to one hundred and two.

Who could have known how sensitive I am to poison ivy? she wondered.

Who could have known how allergic I am?

A week later, Selena's face was still puffy. Her hands and arms were covered with scabs. As she leaned over her geometry text, she found herself scratching the rash that wouldn't go away.

How could I have been so stupid? she asked herself for the hundredth time. *Everyone knows what poison ivy looks like. Was I really that desperate to get flowers from Eddy?*

"How do you feel?" Jake whispered.

"Better, thanks," Selena muttered.

"You *look* better," Katy told her. "A little, anyway."

The three friends were sitting around a small table in the library, where they were assigned for study hall.

"I feel like such an idiot," Selena moaned. "This is the most embarrassing thing I've ever done. I can't believe I had to miss play practice, too!"

"It's not your fault," Jake whispered. "If some creep sends you poison iv—"

"Shh!" Katy warned as the librarian frowned at them.

Selena turned back to her books. A few minutes later, the librarian stepped out into the hall, and Jake nudged her again. "Ready for rehearsal?" he asked. "Only two weeks until opening night!"

"I hope my rash is cleared up by then," Selena moaned.

"I'm not even sure you should do the play," Jake whispered.

"What? Are you serious?" Selena cried.

"I agree with Jake," Katy said somberly.

"But don't you get it?" Selena argued. "That's what he wants me to do—quit the play. I don't want to give him the satisfaction."

"I wish we knew who it was," Katy sighed.

"*I* know who it is," Jake declared. "It's got to be Danny."

Selena made a face. "I don't think so. What makes you so sure?"

"I don't want to say yet," Jake replied. "But I have been doing some checking."

Selena stared at him. "What do you mean, checking?"

"Just asking around, finding things out," he explained. His eyes burned into hers. "I know how much you want that scholarship. I promise I'll find out what's going on."

"Thanks," Selena said sincerely. "But, Jake . . . I know you've been having problems of your own. I don't want you to worry about me."

"Hey," he said, giving her a grin. "What are friends for?"

Selena glanced impatiently at the clock. She could barely wait for the last bell to ring. Her history teacher droned on and on. All she could think about was her conversation with Katy and Jake.

Why was Jake so certain that Danny was the stalker? He had seemed almost happy about it. What did Jake know? Did he know something for sure?

"Selena? You okay?" Katy whispered.

Selena glanced over at her friend. Katy sat next to Selena in the back row of the classroom. Selena nodded and picked up her pen to take notes.

But as soon as Katy looked away, Selena's mind returned to Jake and Danny.

Jake might be fooling himself, Selena thought unhappily. *He* wants *Danny to be the stalker. He doesn't know for sure.*

She gnawed on her pen. *I appreciate Jake trying to help me. But I should try to find the creep myself. I can't let Jake do my dirty work.*

Selena saw Katy staring at her again. Quickly she began taking notes to cover her nervousness.

Maybe there's some kind of clue in the stage area, she thought. *Something that will show me who the stalker is.*

The final bell rang, making Selena jump.

She knew what she had to do.

Why didn't I do this weeks ago? she wondered as she rushed out of the classroom. She was halfway to the auditorium when Katy caught up to her.

"Selena, wait!" she called. "Want a ride home?"

"Thanks, Katy," Selena replied. "But I've got something to do first. I'll catch the bus later."

"Sure? I don't mind waiting."

Selena hesitated. Should she tell Katy where she was going? She felt funny about what she planned to do. Snooping around other people's stuff . . .

"You go ahead," she told Katy.

Selena made sure no one saw her as she entered the auditorium. *I'm not snooping,* she told herself. *I'm just protecting myself.*

She climbed onto the stage and searched around. Everything appeared normal. She crossed to where the curtain ropes were tied. Again, she saw nothing unusual.

Selena sighed. She pulled open the backstage door and hurried to the locker room. This was where cast and crew members kept their personal things. This was where she might find something— anything—that would lead her to the creep who had been threatening her.

She glanced around. Except for a pile of costumes and props on the table in the corner, the room stood empty. The battered metal lockers were never locked. Selena edged toward them.

She opened her own locker first, and found it empty except for a white hair band she thought she had lost. She picked it up and absently placed it in her pocket.

Then she opened the next locker, which belonged to Alison. Empty.

"This is ridiculous," Selena told herself aloud.

"I don't even know what I'm looking for."

She opened two more lockers at random, then quickly shut them. None of them contained anything except a few items of clothing.

Selena crossed the room and peered at the cast bulletin board. Her eye fell on the list of locker assignments tacked to one corner. She quickly scanned the list, then returned to the row of lockers.

She knew why she had really come here. She wanted to look inside Danny's locker. She had no proof that he was the stalker. But she hadn't been able to think of anyone else. And Jake kept saying it must be Danny.

Selena simply had to know.

Locker number 111.

Selena stared at it for a moment, feeling guilty. She took a deep breath, then quickly yanked the door open.

At first she thought the locker was empty. She started to slam the door shut again.

But then she saw something stuck in the back of the locker. A small, shiny square of paper. Selena reached for it. Examined it.

And uttered a low cry as she realized what she held.

A page of stickers.

Most of the page had been peeled away. But at

the bottom she saw at least a dozen orange suns.

Selena stared down at the stickers, feeling sick.

Danny.

Danny was the one, after all.

Danny. Danny. Danny.

To think she had once been so close with him. She had been so crazy about him.

She stepped back. Her legs felt rubbery. Her mouth suddenly felt dry.

She read the number again. Locker number 111. Danny's locker.

Selena gripped the stickers tightly in her hand. Her heart raced.

Don't jump to conclusions, she told herself. *Make sure you have the right person.*

She returned to the bulletin board to double-check the locker number. She quickly scanned the names. There it was: Danny Morris—number 112.

Huh?

112?

No!

No! She had opened locker number 111!

Selena returned to the list. The columns of numbers made her dizzy. She used her finger to draw a line from number 111.

Carefully she ran her finger across the wrinkled paper.

And gasped as she read the correct name.
She read the name again. Then once more.
She couldn't make herself believe it.
Locker 111 belonged to Jake. Jake Jacoby.
Jake was the stalker. The Sun.

20

Selena stared at the sheet of stickers, then back at the list of lockers. No mistake. The stickers had been in Jake's locker.

She felt numb. Could it be true?

She had known Jake her whole life. They'd been good friends since kindergarten. How could Jake have written those terrible notes? How could he threaten her?

Why would he threaten her?

Had Jake tried to hurt her? Had he pushed the wardrobe over on Alison? Sent the spotlights plunging down? Tried to run her down in that dark car?

No! a part of Selena screamed. *No, no, no!*

Jake could never do those things. He could never hurt her. He could never hurt anyone.

But then, why were the stickers in his locker?

If it is Jake, she realized, *then I don't know him at all. He's sick. Very, very sick.*

She jammed the stickers into her backpack. With a shudder, she hurried out the stage door, into the parking lot behind the school.

The sky had darkened. Selena glanced at her watch and saw that she had spent more time backstage than she'd thought. The last bus had long since left.

Oh well, she thought. *I'll walk home.* It was a long walk, but it would give her a chance to think.

As she hurried along Park Drive, she tried to decide what to do.

Why was Jake doing these things to her?

She thought about his attitude toward Danny. Was Jake jealous of Danny? Was Jake jealous of what Danny had meant to Selena?

If Jake wanted to go out with me, why didn't he just ask me?

It didn't make sense. She knew she had to confront him.

He'll have an explanation, she told herself. *Maybe there's a perfectly logical reason for the sun stickers in his locker.*

Right. And maybe there's really an Easter Bunny.

By the time Selena reached home, she knew

what to do. She planned to call Jake and tell him what she had found. She would demand an explanation—and he would give her one.

Simple. She hoped.

Selena dumped her backpack on the bed and reached for the phone. It rang before she picked it up. Selena jumped in surprise.

"Hello?" she asked sharply.

"Hi, Selena," Katy chirped. "What's up?"

"Oh, Katy," Selena moaned.

"Selena?" Katy cried. "What's wrong?"

"Remember when you and I and—and Jake— were talking about the stalker? And Jake said he was going to prove it was Danny?"

"Yeah?" Katy prompted.

"Well, I felt bad that Jake kept worrying about me. So I decided to snoop around myself."

"And?" Katy asked.

"And I . . . I went backstage after school," Selena recounted. "I searched through the lockers. And I found a sheet of sun stickers!"

Katy gasped. "Like the ones that were on the notes?"

"Exactly like them," Selena confirmed. "And about half of the stickers are missing."

"Wow," Katy breathed. "That proves it's Danny!"

"It's not Danny," Selena almost sobbed. "I didn't find them in *his* locker." She could feel her voice shaking and took a deep breath to steady herself.

"Well?" Katy demanded. "Whose locker was it?"

"Jake's," Selena choked out. "I found them in Jake's locker."

For a moment Katy didn't say anything. "No way," she finally murmured. "I don't believe it."

"Me neither," Selena agreed. "But it's true!"

"Jake wouldn't do anything like that," Katy protested. "I mean, he's always been a joker, but he's never done anything mean."

"There's only one explanation that makes sense," Selena decided. "Jake *was* joking. It was all some kind of goof."

"Some goof," Katy groaned. "Alison ended up in the hospital. I still have a deep bruise from the spotlight bar hitting my arm."

"I know," Selena said. "That's why it had to be a joke. Jake couldn't hurt a fly—you know that. Those must have really been accidents. He didn't mean for anyone to get hurt."

"What about the poison ivy?" Katy demanded.

"Maybe he didn't know it was poison ivy," Selena suggested. She sighed. "Pretty lame, huh? I just don't want it to be Jake."

"I know," Katy replied sincerely. "I don't either."

"In any case, I have to give him a chance to explain, don't I?" Selena asked.

"I don't know." Katy suddenly sounded frightened. "Before you talk to Jake, maybe you should confide in someone else. Tell Mr. Riordan or maybe the police."

"No!" Selena cried. "I don't want Jake to get in trouble. If he hurt Alison—even by accident—he'll get kicked out of school! Or even worse. I can't do that to him!"

"Selena, anyone can become mentally ill," Katy argued. "If Jake is sick, you should get him help."

"I don't think he's sick," Selena protested. "I think he was kidding!"

"Think of how moody he's been lately," Katy returned. "And how he keeps picking fights with Danny. Maybe he couldn't hurt anyone before, but you've seen him try to hurt Danny."

Selena didn't know what to say. Katy was right—Jake had been acting strangely. And he had definitely started fights with Danny.

"I still can't believe—" At that moment Selena heard a call-waiting *click* on the phone. "Hang on, Katy," she said.

Selena clicked to the other line.

"Selena?" came a familiar voice. "It's Jake."

Selena felt her throat close up. She thought of what Katy had said. What if Jake hadn't been joking?

"Selena? Are you there?"

"Hi, Jake," she finally managed to choke out.

"I have to see you," he said. His voice sounded so urgent. Almost desperate.

"Okay," Selena answered. "I need to talk to you, too."

"In person," Jake said breathlessly. "I've got to talk to you in person. As soon as possible."

Selena's heart began to race. "Can't we just talk on the phone?" she asked.

"No, it's too complicated," Jake replied. "Please, Moon? It's important."

"Jake, I know about the stickers," Selena blurted out.

"What?"

"I found them, Jake. In your locker backstage."

She heard a sigh on the other end of the line. "I can explain that," he told her. "I found out the truth about the stalker, Selena. I'm at school now. Can you meet me in the auditorium?"

"Jake, why can't you tell me over the—"

"No!" he interrupted. "I have to show you some things. Meet me here, Selena. Right away."

"But, Jake—"

"I'll wait for you," he said.

She heard a hollow *click* as he hung up.

She clicked back to the other line. "Katy?"

"What's wrong?" Katy asked immediately. "You sound upset."

"It was Jake," Selena murmured. "He wants me to meet him at school. Will you come with me?"

"You mean now?"

"Yes."

"Sure," Katy agreed. "I'll pick you up in ten minutes."

"Thanks," Selena breathed, hanging up the phone.

She quickly drank a glass of cold water from the refrigerator. Then she slipped on her jacket and waited for Katy to arrive. She was staring out the front window when the phone rang again.

"Selena?" It was Katy. "I'm really sorry, but I can't come. I forgot. My mom took my car while hers is in the shop. She's not home. And I promised to stay home and wait for a package to be delivered."

"That's okay," Selena replied, trying to hide her disappointment. "I can take the bus."

"I feel terrible."

"Don't worry about it. I can handle Jake."

"Well, okay," Katy agreed reluctantly. "Call me as soon as you get home."

"I will. Don't worry. Jake says he can explain. Everything will be fine."

Selena tried to stay calm on the bus ride back to school. She took deep breaths, watched the cars and shops outside, and did her best to keep her mind distracted.

It didn't work. She couldn't stop thinking about the stickers. About the threats. About Jake.

He had been so insistent on the phone. So insistent about meeting her in person. Was it really because he wanted to show her something?

Or was it because he wanted to try to hurt her again?

Selena leaned her head against the bus window and pictured Jake's horrible fight with Danny. *Maybe I should have paid more attention to the way he's been acting*, she thought. *I should have been a better friend, given him more attention.*

She glanced nervously at her watch. The bus pulled up across the street from the high school, and Selena hopped off.

It was a cold, moonless night, and she shivered, pulling her jacket tighter.

She glanced around the side of the school. A few teachers' cars were still in the teachers' parking lot. No sign of anyone else.

The auditorium was in the back of the big

old building. Lights near the office told her that the custodian was working in the front part of the school.

The stage door was propped open with a brick. There didn't seem to be any light inside.

If only Katy could have come with me, Selena thought.

There was no putting it off. She had to go in. *Jake's my friend,* she told herself. *One of my oldest friends in the world. There's no way he'd hurt me. No way.*

She felt around on the wall until she found the backstage light, and switched it on. "Jake?" she called. "Jake, are you here?"

No answer. Just the echo of her voice off the auditorium walls.

Maybe he's not even here, she thought suddenly. *Maybe this is another joke. I bet he's sitting at home laughing, wondering how long I'll wait for him.*

"Jake?" she called again, more loudly this time.

Still no answer.

Selena began to relax.

She moved out to the auditorium and switched on the houselights. All the seats were empty.

"Very funny, Jake," she said aloud. "You're a real riot."

She returned to the stage. Someone had left a script on a stool by the stage door.

She picked it up and glanced at the name scrawled across the top. Jake's name.

Jake's script.

He *did* come here, Selena realized. Was he still somewhere in the auditorium? Was this part of a trap?

All Selena's fears rushed back into her mind. "Jake?" she called again. "Where are you?"

She glanced around the stage area, but saw only props and folded clothes.

Maybe he's in the locker room, she thought. She crossed to the backstage door and poked her head through. The locker room appeared empty.

He must have left his script here earlier this afternoon, Selena thought. She didn't really care anymore. She only wanted to get home. Only wanted to forget about this strange day.

She returned to the door and was about to switch the lights off when something caught her eye.

A bundle of clothes piled beneath the ladder to the catwalk.

That's odd, Selena thought. *Who left a costume on the floor?*

Puzzled, she stepped forward to take a closer look.

Selena's breath caught in her throat.

The clothes didn't look right. A costume wouldn't lie so stiffly.

And she saw sneakers. And jeans.

Not a costume, Selena realized. Not a costume.

A person.

A person, crumpled in a heap. Crumpled on the stage.

Arms bent under the body. Head snapped to the side. One leg pointed at an impossible angle.

A body like a fallen marionette.

Glassy puppet eyes staring up at her.

"Jake?"

The name escaped her lips in a whisper.

"Jake?"

21

H e fell off the catwalk," Selena uttered, feeling numb. Feeling dazed. As if the words she spoke into the phone receiver had no meaning, made no sense. "He broke his neck. The police said it was an accident."

"I just can't believe it!" Katy's voice trembled on the other end of the line. "What was Jake doing up on the catwalk?"

"No one knows," Selena replied. Then she added in a whisper: "No one will ever know."

She shuddered as she remembered the way Jake's blank, lifeless eyes had stared up at her. She remembered screaming and tearing at her hair. For how long? She didn't know. The school custodian found her slumped against the wall near Jake's body.

"Oh, Selena." Katy sighed, "I feel so bad. I'm

sorry I wasn't with you when you found him. I still can't believe . . ." Katy's voice trailed off. She let out a sob.

"I—I can't talk anymore," Selena choked out. "I had to call you, Katy. I know it's really late. The police kept me there for hours."

"I don't care what time it is," Katy cried. "Is your mom home?"

"No. She's at work. I'll tell her when she gets home. She'll be very upset, too."

"I'll come over if you want," Katy offered. "I don't think you should be alone."

"I *want* to be alone," Selena answered. "Thanks anyway."

Katy's voice came out tiny and soft, like a little girl's. "You sure?"

"Yeah. Thanks. Good night."

"See you tomorrow," Katy replied in a whisper.

Selena hung up the phone and stared at the receiver. *Will my life ever be normal again?* she wondered. *Will I ever get used to Jake not being around?*

At least I don't have to be afraid anymore, she thought.

The stalker is dead.

Jake. Jake. Jake. His name repeated in her mind until it became a meaningless chant.

Jake, why did you threaten me?

Jake, why did you hate me so much?

Play rehearsals were postponed till the end of the week. Selena stayed home from school most of the week. Her mom wanted her to get over the shock instead of pretending that everything was normal. As Selena entered the auditorium on Friday afternoon, she felt strange, almost as if she were an intruder.

What's wrong with me? she wondered. *The stage is where I belong. Why don't I feel comfortable here?*

She sensed that everyone else felt strange too. Even Danny acted less obnoxious than usual. "Hey, Selena," he said gently. "I'm sorry about Jake. I know how close you were."

"Thanks, Danny," Selena murmured.

"How are you feeling?" Katy asked sympathetically.

"I feel so sad, Katy," Selena replied. "I still can't believe that Jake wanted to hurt me. I wish . . . I wish I had a chance to talk to him before . . . the accident."

"I know," Katy agreed. "I keep thinking of when we were little. Remember that old tree house in Jake's yard? We were such good friends then. Nothing ever came between us."

"That was fun," Selena replied. "I always had

the best times in my life with you and Jake."

"Places, everyone!" Mr. Riordan called.

When all the cast members had gathered, he cleared his throat and stared gravely at them. "Our theater family has suffered a terrible tragedy," he announced dramatically. "We'll all miss Jake. But—as Jake himself would have agreed—the show must go on!"

Is that all there is to it? Selena wondered. *Does the show really have to go on—no matter what happens?*

Mr. Riordan directed them to begin. Selena took a deep breath and prepared to speak her lines.

But it didn't seem to work. When Danny uttered Romeo's words, she saw Jake's face. When the boy who had taken Jake's role spoke his lines, Selena imagined Jake in his place.

During a break, she wandered backstage. She wondered why Eddy hadn't come to rehearsal today.

Selena had only spoken to him once since Jake's death. She hadn't told him that Jake was the stalker.

She couldn't bear to think about it.

Katy sat backstage on a prop table, looking nearly as glum as Selena felt. "How's it going?" Katy asked. "What are you doing back here?"

Selena frowned. "I just can't get into it."

"I know what you mean. I've messed up the lighting cues three times. The stage manager is ready to kill me."

"I keep thinking the show must go on," Selena continued. "But I don't get it. *Why* should we keep doing the dumb play? Jake is dead! That's more important than a play. I wish I'd realized that earlier. Maybe Jake would still be alive."

"You can't blame yourself," Katy replied softly.

"I can't help it!" Selena cried. "I understand it now. When Jake wrote those notes, he was trying to get me to stop taking the plays so seriously. They're all I ever thought about."

Katy nodded. "Maybe so."

"I guess he thought if he scared me, I'd give it up. But I didn't pay attention to him. I should have listened."

"Places!" Mr. Riordan called from the front of the auditorium. "Selena? Where is Selena?"

Selena started toward the curtain. She didn't know if she would have the strength to finish this rehearsal. Every time she thought of Jake, she wanted to cry. *No play is worth dying for,* she thought. *And no scholarship is worth losing a friend for.*

She stopped and turned back to Katy. "You know what? I've made a big decision."

22

Mr. Riordan," Selena called, "I need to tell you
something. It's important."

The rehearsal had just ended, and the
teacher was stuffing his script into a leather brief-
case. "Not now, Selena," he answered, straightening
up. "I'm already late."

"It won't take long—" Selena promised.

"Sorry," Mr. Riordan called, striding to the
door. "Catch me tomorrow morning. You were great
tonight, by the way!"

"But—"

"See you tomorrow." With a brusque wave, Mr.
Riordan disappeared through the door.

"Did you tell him? Did you tell him you're
leaving the play?" Katy's voice startled Selena. She
hadn't heard her friend approach.

"No," she answered unhappily. "He was in

some kind of a super rush." Selena ran a shaky hand through her hair. "I can't stand it, Katy," she moaned. "I'm so jumpy. I should feel safer now that I know the stalker is gone, right? But everything about this play still feels wrong."

"Well, I think you're doing the right thing," Katy replied. "Getting out of this play will be good for you. It will take your mind off Jake."

"I know," Selena agreed. "If only Mr. Riordan had let me tell him tonight."

"Tell him what?" a voice demanded.

Selena turned to see Danny standing behind her. Instead of his usual smirk, he wore a concerned expression.

"Wow. Danny," Selena said. "I didn't know you were there."

"I saw you two talking, so I thought I'd join you," he said. "You were excellent tonight, Selena."

"Danny, please—" Selena started.

"No. I mean it," he insisted. "I thought you were really brave to go on. I mean, after what happened to Jake."

"Yeah, right," Selena muttered.

"What were you going to tell Mr. Riordan?" Danny demanded.

"It's nothing." Selena lowered her eyes to the floor.

"Tell him, Selena," Katy urged. "He'll find out sooner or later anyway."

"I guess so," Selena agreed. She took a deep breath. "I'm quitting the play," she announced.

Danny's mouth dropped open in surprise. He narrowed his eyes at Selena. "This is a joke, right?" he asked.

"No," Selena assured him. "I'm serious. I think it's what Jake would have wanted."

"Are you totally nuts?" Danny exclaimed. "You're going to quit the play because of an accident?"

Selena nodded but didn't reply. To her surprise, her announcement made Danny angry.

"Oh, I get it," he said unpleasantly. "You just can't stand it, can you, Selena? You can't stand not being the center of attention. Since Jake's accident, everyone is talking about him, not you. So you have to do something to get the attention back to you."

Selena gasped. She felt as if he'd slapped her. "What a gross thing to say! You are the crudest, most obnoxious—"

"It's the truth!" Danny insisted bitterly.

"Leave her alone, Danny!" Katy cried.

"Why should I?" he exploded. "This is so typical! Selena is the star. We can't have the play without Selena. Selena is upset. Selena is frightened,"

Danny ranted. "Well, you know what, Selena? Everyone's getting a little sick of your selfishness. If you quit, you'll hurt a lot of people."

Selena stared at him, tears in her eyes. She had never expected him to attack her this way. She hadn't even thought about what would happen if she quit.

"But you don't care about the rest of us, do you?" he went on. "All you care about is yourself. What makes *you* comfortable. What's important to *you.* You've really changed—"

"I said leave her alone!" Katy yelled. She tugged at Danny's jacket.

But he paid no attention to her. He glared at Selena. "Do you know what will happen if you drop out of the play? It will be canceled, that's what! Nobody else can play Juliet but Alison, and she's still in a neck brace! All the work the rest of us did will be wasted. All because of you."

"Stop it!" Katy yelled. "Can't you see how bad Selena feels? She wants to quit! It's not her fault there's no other Juliet!"

"What about the other seniors in the play?" Danny continued. "For some of us, it's the last chance ever to be on stage, Selena. We're not all going off to acting school, you know."

Selena's head spun. She hadn't thought about

anything except how much she missed Jake.

She turned to Katy, who stood in front of her like a protective bulldog. "He's right," Selena said softly. "I can't quit the play now. It would hurt too many people. I wasn't thinking."

"But—" Katy started.

"It's okay," Selena assured her. "I can do it. It won't kill me to do the play."

Selena gazed at the glowing numbers on her digital clock. It was 3:02 a.m. She stretched and yawned. Something had awakened her. A noise.

She listened hard. Silence now.

She turned over, but her eyes didn't want to close.

I'll have a glass of ice water, she decided. That always helped her relax. She tiptoed downstairs to the kitchen. She drank a few swallows of water from the bottle. She was about to replace it in the refrigerator when something caught her eye.

Something white.

In the crack underneath the kitchen door.

A piece of paper.

Another note!

Don't be ridiculous, Selena scolded herself. *This can't be from the stalker. Jake was the stalker, and he is dead.*

A feeling of dread tightened Selena's stomach as she bent down to retrieve the note.

She raised it into the rectangle of light from the open refrigerator.

Saw the printed letters. And the orange sun sticker at the bottom.

And knew that the stalker was still alive.

23

Dear Selena,
Surprise!
You thought you had it all figured out.
But you were wrong. Dead wrong.
Jake was wrong too. That's why he
had to die.
I'm still watching you. I'll be in your
audience at the dress rehearsal.
Poor Juliet. She died such a horrible
death.
Poor Selena, too.
The Sun

Selena turned the note over and over in her hands. She held her breath, waiting for her body to stop trembling.

Then she shut the kitchen door, fastened the

chain latch, locked the bolt, and gazed out into the yard.

The trees of the Fear Street Woods cast long, slender shadows into her backyard. Was he out there? Was The Sun hiding in the woods somewhere? Watching her?

She turned away from the window, feeling cold and numb.

Jake was not The Sun.

She thought back to the last conversation she'd had with him. It seemed like a hundred years ago.

Meet me at the auditorium, he had told her. *I found out the truth about the stalker.*

Whatever he found out had meant his death.

The Sun had killed Jake.

The Sun wasn't joking. He really was a murderer.

And now he was going to kill Selena.

I won't give in to him, she vowed. *I'm going to finish this play for Jake. And I'll find out who The Sun is. I'll find out and see that he is caught.*

The Sun had said he'd be watching the dress rehearsal. So Selena decided to watch for him. Maybe he would do something to give himself away.

I should be scared, Selena thought as she

began to button the linen, high-necked blouse of her Juliet costume. *But I'm not. I'm too angry to be scared. The Sun is out there. And I'm going to figure out who he is.*

"Selena?" a familiar voice brought her out of her thoughts.

"Oh, hi, Alison."

"How's it going?" Alison asked. "Need any help with your hair?" Alison wore the black coveralls of a stagehand, her neck brace covered with a dark scarf.

"I'm almost ready," Selena replied. "I just need a little more hair spray."

"Break a leg," Alison said softly. "I know how hard this rehearsal must be for you."

"Thanks." Selena smiled. "But the show must go on, right?"

She finished her hair, then joined Mr. Riordan and some of the others in a corner of the backstage area.

"We have a good-size audience," Mr. Riordan told them. "I invited some of the coaches, and most of the football team is here."

"You're kidding!" Katy laughed.

"It seemed like a good idea," he replied. "A good way to fill the house in the afternoon."

Selena peeked through the curtain. Half of the seats were filled—the biggest audience they'd ever had for a dress rehearsal.

How am I going to find The Sun? she wondered, studying the faces.

"Break a leg, Selena," a husky voice whispered in her ear. She spun around to see Eddy grinning at her, his eyes flashing excitedly.

"Thanks," she murmured. "Aren't you going to watch?"

"I wish I could," he told her, his smile fading. "But I have a class this afternoon. I'm sure you'll do a great job, though."

"I wish you could stay," she told him sincerely. "I'm so nervous."

"I know you still feel bad about Jake," he said. "But you won't let that affect your performance. You're too good for that."

Selena stared at him. She really didn't want him to leave. She needed to talk to him. She needed him to be there watching her.

"Places!" Mr. Riordan's shout interrupted.

Eddy rushed offstage. The other actors swarmed around Selena. She calmed herself by taking several slow, deep breaths.

I'm ready, she thought.

Ready to become Juliet.

For the last time, said a voice in her head.

Unless you find The Sun.

"Curtain!" Mr. Riordan called.

The rehearsal went well. Once the play started,

Selena forgot about The Sun and her fear. When-ever she performed, she forgot about her Selena-self, as she called it, and felt herself inhabiting the character. Her Juliet-self.

Even the fact that her Romeo was Danny Morris didn't interfere with her performance. While she was acting, she felt that she *was* Juliet, desperately in love with Romeo.

She was dimly aware of the audience, some-times laughing, sometimes murmuring. As the cur-tain went down for the last time, applause filled the auditorium.

The curtain went up again.

As Selena bowed, she imagined that Jake was on the stage beside her.

He should be here, Selena thought. *This play is for him. And I'll never quit acting. I'll dedicate all my performances to Jake. My life would have no meaning if I quit acting.*

Standing next to her, Danny took hold of her hand and squeezed. She tried to pull away, but he held on tighter.

"Cut it out!" she growled out of the side of her mouth. But he continued to grasp her hand.

As soon as the curtain dropped again, she angrily yanked her hand away from him. "Let me go!" she shouted.

"Hey, I was just staying in character," Danny protested.

"Well, you can get out of it right now!" She stormed away.

She waved to Mr. Riordan. "Good show!" he called, looking up from his clipboard. "I'll have notes for everyone after school tomorrow."

Selena hurried to the backstage locker room. She'd promised her mother she'd get home early and help with some chores.

She ignored the excited voices and laughter of the other drama club members. She changed her outfit. Then she searched for her backpack. The kids all tossed their backpacks against the back wall.

Selena grabbed up each one, then dropped it back to the floor. *I'm going to miss the bus,* she thought. *Where is my backpack?*

"Oh!" She remembered she had left it in her locker in the front of the building.

"Hey, Selena—!"

She heard Katy calling to her. "No time!" Selena called back. She ran to the hallway and headed at full speed toward her locker all the way on the other side of the building.

Breathing hard, she fumbled with the lock. Finally pulled the locker open. What a disaster area! She'd been meaning to clean it out for weeks.

She pulled out the backpack. Frantically shoved books and papers from the locker floor inside. Slammed the locker. Locked it. And ran to the bus stop.

She didn't check the contents of the backpack until after dinner. She went up to her room, planning to do her homework. The backpack was jammed so full, she couldn't find anything she needed.

So she dumped everything out on the bed.

And saw the square white envelope. The square white envelope with the sticker of the orange sun in the corner.

Another note.

With a cry of disgust, Selena tore open the envelope and quickly scanned the ugly message:

> *Dear Selena,*
> *How did you like my new surprise?*
> *Bet you never guessed I'd kill another*
> *one. Another person close to you. In*
> *the same place, too.*
> *You should have listened to me. But*
> *you did the play anyway. So it's not*
> *my fault. It's yours.*
> *I told you I would be at dress*
> *rehearsal, Selena. It was the perfect*
> *time to kill someone.*

I'll be at opening night, too. It will be
the perfect time to kill you.
The Sun
Selena stared at the note, unable to
breathe, unable to move.

Someone else killed?
Who?

24

Killed someone? Killed someone?

Selena read the note again, her pulse racing, the words flashing as she squinted at them.

What on earth was The Sun talking about? He claimed he'd "killed another one."

But no one had been killed. Or even hurt.

Selena forced her mind to focus. The Sun said he had killed someone in the auditorium. Killed someone as he had killed Jake. At dress rehearsal.

But dress rehearsal had been over for hours.

And it had gone perfectly smoothly.

No one had died. No one. No one. No one . . .

"Ohhh!" Selena let out a moan of horror as she realized what had happened.

The note . . . it had been shoved into her locker in the front hall. The stalker didn't think she'd go back to that locker.

He had left the note there for her to see tomorrow morning.

She wasn't supposed to receive this note until tomorrow.

A chill crept down Selena's spine as she understood.

She wasn't supposed to see this note until after The Sun had killed whoever he was planning to kill.

Until after tonight.

She felt sick. Someone was in terrible danger.

Tonight. *Now.*

Because of her.

I have to go back to school! she decided. *I've got to stop him.*

And then she had an even more chilling thought. The Sun was threatening to kill someone close to her. There weren't many people left.

Katy.

No—please! I can't let him kill Katy!

Selena grabbed up the phone and punched in Katy's number. One ring. Two. Three.

"Come on, Katy. Pick it up! Pick it up!"

No one home.

Katy is probably back at school working on the lights, Selena realized. *Yes. Katy must be there. She's walking into a trap.*

She grabbed her jacket and started out of her room.

The phone rang. Selena grabbed it quickly. *Please be Katy,* she prayed.

"Selena? It's Eddy."

"Eddy!" she exclaimed. Ordinarily she would have been happy to hear his voice. But not now. Not now.

"Are you okay?" he asked.

"Yeah. But I don't have time—"

"You sound upset," he interrupted. "I won't keep you. I just called to say I'm sorry I couldn't watch your rehearsal this afternoon."

"That's okay," Selena said, scarcely listening.

"So how did it go?"

"What? Oh, the rehearsal. It went great," she told him impatiently. "I've really got to go—"

"Fine," he replied. "But I'd like to see you tonight. Are you busy later? It's seven now. Could I meet you at eight?"

"I—" Selena didn't know how to answer. "I don't know. There's something I have to do."

"Can I help?"

"I wish you could," Selena declared. "But no one can help. I have to go."

"Okay," Eddy replied, his voice disappointed. "But—"

"I've got to go *now*," Selena repeated. "Bye."

She hung up the phone, feeling guilty—and afraid. *Maybe I should have told Eddy what's going on,* she thought. *But I can't trust him. I can't trust anybody!*

She shut her eyes tightly and tried to calm down.

Katy. Katy is in danger because of me. I can't let him hurt her. Whoever he is.

She grabbed her jacket and hurried out the door.

The Shadyside High parking lot stood empty except for the custodian's van. Selena didn't see a single light shining from the building.

She pulled a pocket flashlight from her backpack and crossed the parking lot to the back of the school. The heavy double doors of the auditorium appeared dark and forbidding.

Selena glanced over her shoulder. *I'd feel better if there were cars here,* she thought. *Is The Sun already here? Is he waiting for his victim?*

At least Katy's car wasn't in the student lot. *Maybe Katy isn't here,* Selena hoped. *Maybe the stage crew isn't working tonight.*

The doors were shut, but not locked. She pulled them open. Selena stepped inside the darkened auditorium, moving as silently as she could. She switched on the flashlight and swung it around.

Empty. No one here.

No one in the seats. No one on the stage.

Was Katy up on the catwalk, working on the lights? Trying to stay calm, she called out. "Katy? Are you here?"

No answer.

And then Selena heard a sound that made her gasp and drop the flashlight.

A muffled scream. Coming from behind the closed curtain.

"Katy?" she called again. "Katy? Katy? Is that you?"

25

"Katy?"

No answer.

Selena grabbed the back of a chair. And listened.

Silence now. No scream. No cry. No sound.

Get out of here! screamed a voice in Selena's head. *Turn around and run!*

Katy is in danger because of me, Selena reminded herself.

Did she hear someone behind the curtain? She had no choice. She had to find out.

She picked up the flashlight and slid it into her jeans pocket. Then she began to move through the blackened auditorium. It was so dark that she could barely make out the stage ahead of her. She tiptoed down the center aisle, scarcely daring to breathe, her ears alert for any sound.

Moving carefully, silently, Selena reached the stage and climbed the steps. She peeked through the curtains, straining to see something, anything.

For a moment she considered turning on an overhead light. But she didn't want to give The Sun an advantage. Instead, she switched the little plastic flashlight back on.

"Katy?" she called softly, hearing her own voice tremble. "Katy, it's Selena!"

Still no answer.

She pushed through the curtains. Holding her breath, she shone her light around the backstage area. Again she saw nothing.

Selena let the beam of light explore the stage. Empty. No one here.

Not a sound. Not a sound . . .

Until she reached the very back of the stage.

And heard a moan, so faint that she had to strain to make it out.

"Katy?" she called again. "Where are you?"

Another moan. From above?

Selena swung the beam of yellow light up toward the catwalk. But the flashlight wasn't powerful enough to reach that high.

At the top of the metal ladder stood the small prop room that led out onto the catwalk. Selena knew it was up there, but she had never seen it.

Her fear of heights kept her from climbing that ladder.

She moved closer to the ladder. Something shiny glinted on the floor beneath it.

Selena swung her flashlight beam toward the spot. What shone so darkly there on the floor? A puddle.

A dark red puddle. Red as blood.

Selena jumped back as she heard another moan from above.

The moan of someone in pain.

And then the words, so faint, so faint that Selena could barely hear them: "Help me . . . someone . . . please help me!"

26

Selena gazed up at the catwalk. It was very high, she saw, feeling a cold shudder run down her back. So high and steep. Straight up.

Katy had never been afraid to climb the ladder. Selena had tried to climb it once. On a dare from Jake. She had made it halfway to the top. Then she felt so dizzy and sick that she had to climb back down.

"Ohhhhh." The moan again.

"I'm coming!" Selena called. She shoved the flashlight back into her jeans pocket. Firmly gripping the ladder with both hands, she began to climb.

One step after another.

Don't look down, she told herself.

She climbed higher, higher still. She felt the familiar panic fill her chest. For a moment the dark walls spun around her. She stopped, shut her eyes, and hugged the ladder as tightly as she could.

I can't go any higher, she thought.

You have to, she urged herself. *This time you have to.*

She took another step up.

Her stomach churned. Cold sweat beaded her face.

Don't think of how high it is, she thought. *Just concentrate on each step. One at a time.*

After what seemed like hours, Selena reached the top of the ladder. She leaned into it, gripping firmly with her right hand. Then she used her left hand to pull out the flashlight and click it on.

The beam of light revealed the prop room leading onto the catwalk.

The door was shut.

Selena saw no sign of Katy. No sign of anyone.

"Katy!" she called, her voice choked with panic.

"Where are you?"

Silence.

Selena glanced down. A wave of dizziness swept over her. For a moment, her grip on the ladder loosened and she knew she would fall.

I have to get off this ladder, she thought. *Then I'll decide what to do.*

Gripping the ladder tightly with one hand,

she pulled the prop room door open with the other. Then she stepped off the ladder and threw herself into the room. Trembling, she slammed the door shut and leaned against the wall.

The prop room was dark. For a moment Selena saw nothing. Slowly her eyes focused on a sliver of light seeping under another door. The door that led onto the catwalk.

I'm safe for now, Selena told herself. *I'll worry about how to get back down later.*

"Katy?" she whispered into the darkness. "Are you here?"

No answer.

Selena shone the light around the tiny room. She was surprised at how full it was, the rows of shelves crammed with props and costumes.

One large storage cabinet divided the room in half. Selena crawled toward it. She heard a scraping sound from the other side of the room.

"Hey—!" She spun around. "Who is there?" she cried hoarsely.

Her question was answered by another moan.

Selena crawled closer to the cabinet.

She leaned around it.

And found herself face-to-face with Danny Morris.

27

Selena opened her mouth in a terrified scream.

I'm trapped, she realized. *Danny has trapped me up here!*

He stared silently at her.

"Danny!" she cried. "Danny?"

Now she noticed that he wasn't moving. That his eyes were only half open. That he didn't blink.

Selena gaped at him, her brain spinning in confusion. "Danny . . . ?"

His jaw slid open and he uttered a soft moan.

She raised the beam of light to Danny's face and leaned closer to him. He sat propped against the cabinet, his arms and legs tied by thick ropes.

An ugly purple bruise spread across his forehead. And his blond hair was caked and matted with blood.

"Danny!" Selena gasped. "What happened? Who did this?"

Danny's eyes fluttered open. "Selena?" he murmured.

"What's going on?" she demanded. "Who tied you up?"

"You asked me to come," he choked out.

"Huh? I *what*?" Selena cried, confused. "What happened to you? Who did this?"

"I don't know," Danny groaned. "I came up here because you told me to. You said to wait. I don't remember any more. Why did you ask me to wait for you up here?"

"I—I didn't!" Selena stammered. "I didn't call you!"

"Untie me," he pleaded. "Please."

"Of course," Selena replied. She reached for the ropes. Her hand stopped in midair.

Danny couldn't *be The Sun—could he?*

No way he hit himself over the head and tied himself up! She stared at him. His eyes had closed. Blood dripped thickly from the cut under his hair down the side of his face.

Selena caught her breath. The stalker had planned to kill *Danny*. Danny, not Katy. And Selena must have interrupted him before he could finish.

I saved him! she realized. *I saved Danny!*

Then she felt her heart slide up to her throat. The stalker tried to kill Danny. Selena showed up unexpectedly. The creep ran away. And hid.

Hid somewhere in the auditorium?

Was he still here somewhere?

"We've got to get out of here!" Selena cried. She tugged frantically at the heavy, coiled ropes. They didn't budge. "I'll find something to cut you loose," she told him.

"Clippers . . . in the corner," Danny murmured.

Selena stumbled to the corner and searched frantically for the clippers. "They're not here!" she cried.

"Over the door," Danny choked out. Selena felt above the door. No. No clippers. Nothing she could use to cut Danny free.

She began to paw through the props on the lowest shelf.

And then she heard something. Another sound.

The sound of footsteps, echoing on the stage below.

"It's him," she breathed.

"Who?" Danny whispered.

"Shhh!" Selena stopped moving, straining to hear more.

The footsteps moved closer. Right below them.

She heard a metallic clang. The sound of a foot on the ladder. Another clanging footstep.

Selena switched off the flashlight. She felt

sick with fear. In the darkness, she crawled back to Danny and huddled next to him. "Be quiet!" she whispered urgently. "Don't make a sound!"

The steps continued up the ladder. Steady, confident footsteps.

Then a long silence.

The door creaked open.

In the doorway, nearly lost in the darkness, stood a large figure.

The stalker.

28

Selena froze. And stared into the dark doorway.

And heard a familiar voice. "Selena? Is that you?"

Katy. Katy's voice.

"Katy!" Selena cried, almost sobbing with relief.

"What's going on?" Katy asked. "What are you doing up here?"

"I can't explain now—we're in danger," Selena told her. "Did you see anyone down there?"

"No," Katy said. "I didn't look. I left my math book up here. I was doing some problems during breaks in the rehearsal. Should I look for someone else?"

"No! Never mind!" Selena cried. "Danny is here. He's hurt. We have to get help!"

"Huh?" Katy uttered a startled cry. She switched on an overhead light.

Selena blinked at the sudden brightness. She saw that Katy was wearing her black stagehand's outfit. She carried a heavy metal flashlight.

"Danny's really hurt!" Selena told Katy. "We've got to untie him and get help!"

Katy's face twisted in confusion. "Why is he up here?"

"The Sun," Selena explained. Now that she could see the ropes it was easier to get them untied. "The Sun tried to kill him. I think he's still here somewhere. Come on, Katy, help me untie him!"

"Why?" Katy asked. "If he's tied up, he can't cause trouble."

"Don't you get it?" Selena cried impatiently. "Danny isn't The Sun! I found another note. The Sun said he was going to kill someone close to me. He meant Danny—but I thought he meant you!"

"No, he didn't mean me," Katy replied softly, calmly.

"Katy, help me!" Selena cried. "Danny needs a doctor."

"Don't worry about Danny," Katy soothed her. "He won't cause you any more trouble now."

"Selena," Danny moaned.

Selena tugged at the ropes around his arms.

"I said forget Danny!" Katy screamed. She crossed the room in two steps.

Raised her arm.

And brought the flashlight down hard on Danny's head.

His eyes rolled up. His head slumped onto his chest.

"Katy!" Selena gasped in horror. "Why—?"

Katy pushed a pile of costumes to the floor and settled herself on one of the shelves, facing Selena. "I want to talk about you and me, Selena," Katy explained, her eyes burning into Selena's. "I want to talk about our friendship."

Selena felt a shiver roll down her back. "We can talk about anything you want," she answered carefully. "But let's do it down on the ground."

"I'm very comfortable up here," Katy replied coldly. "Aren't you? You should be. We're together again, the way we used to be."

Something buzzed at the back of Selena's mind. She pushed it away, tried to think clearly. "What do you mean?" Selena asked.

"It's like the old days, just you and me. Best friends. Katy and Selena, doing everything together."

Selena sank onto the floor next to Danny. Stared at his unconscious form. Katy had done that. Katy had hit him. "We're still best friends—"

"Not the way we used to be," Katy insisted. "You used to put me first, Selena. The way I always did with you."

"Katy, I don't know what you're talking about."

"Yes, you do."

Selena watched in dismay as Katy reached into her pocket. She pulled out a shiny piece of paper and held it up for Selena to see.

Selena gasped. "No. Ohh . . . no."

Katy held a sheet of stickers.

Stickers of the sun.

29

Where—where did you get those?" Selena whispered.

"They're mine," Katy replied. "Though I did give a few of them away. But you already know that."

"I don't understand," Selena said. "Katy, you—"

Katy nodded. "Yes, it was Katy. Good old Katy. But I knew you'd never suspect me. I knew you'd think it was some guy who was madly in love with you."

Selena felt too shocked to speak. Katy was her best friend. She couldn't possibly be The Sun. "Those notes—they were written by a guy!" she protested.

Katy sneered at her. "You're so easy to fool. I made them sound as if a guy was writing them. I knew you'd never question it. *Every* guy has to fall for you, right?"

"But, Katy—"

"You're so conceited, Selena. It was so easy to convince you that a stalker was following you around. Even when there was an accident, I could make you believe some crazy guy did it! I mean, a ladder falls down and you think you have a stalker! All I had to do was put a sticker on it! It's obvious all you care about is having guys fall at your feet."

"That's not true!" Selena cried.

"Yeah, right," Katy sneered. "Do you have any idea how I've felt for the past two years, Selena? Do you know how it feels to have your best friend treat you like a servant?"

"I never did that!" Selena protested. "You're still my best friend. We were in the drama club together and—"

"Of course we were in the drama club together," Katy yelled. "Like I had a choice! If I didn't join, I wouldn't have a friend at all!"

"Katy," Selena started carefully. "I never meant to hurt you. I always thought you were happy that I was doing so well!"

"Why should I be happy for you?" Katy snapped. "When we were younger, we cared about each other. As equals. But then you got so thin and so popular. Why should that make me happy?"

"Be-because you were my friend," Selena choked out. "I never knew you felt this way."

"That's the whole point," Katy insisted angrily. "If you were a good friend, you would have known. You would have cared. But you don't care about anything except being a star and getting everyone's attention!"

Selena glanced quickly at Danny. He hadn't moved. He couldn't help her. She had to calm Katy down by herself.

"And then you wanted to leave!" Katy ranted. "You never even told me you wanted to go away to college! You thought you could just get a scholarship and take off! I bet you didn't even think about what would happen to me!"

Selena stared hard at her friend, realizing how disturbed Katy was. And as Katy met Selena's gaze, she seemed to deflate. Her eyes lost their fire. Her whole body slumped.

"I thought I could stop you," Katy murmured. "I thought if I could scare you enough, you'd drop out of the play, and we could go back to being friends."

"Oh, Katy," Selena began, reaching to hug her friend.

"But it didn't work!" Katy yelled, pushing Selena away. "You kept on acting! And you kept on seeing all your new friends and boyfriends. You didn't even care if people got hurt! You just wanted your precious scholarship."

Selena's fear dissolved, replaced by anger. "Are you saying you hurt Alison?" she demanded. "On purpose?"

"I didn't mean to hurt her," Katy replied. "I thought you would be sitting there. I wanted to scare you. But it didn't work." She sighed. "I tried everything, Selena."

Selena swallowed hard. "What about Jake?" Selena asked in a whisper, a horrible suspicion growing in her mind. "You didn't—"

"Jake was too nosy," Katy said calmly, coldly. "You should never have told him about the stalker, Selena. It made him start poking around. Then he found the stickers in my locker."

"In *your* locker!"

"You found them in Jake's locker because he took them out of mine! He shouldn't have done that. He made a big mistake. But it made things easy for me."

"What do you mean?" Selena whispered.

Katy sneered. "I persuaded Jake to come up here. Nobody is as comfortable up here as I am. He didn't have a chance."

"You . . . you pushed him?"

"I couldn't let him tell you what he found out

about me!" Katy replied. "Afterward, I felt sad. I mean, Jake had been a good friend of ours all those years. But things change, Selena." Katy rose quickly to her feet.

Selena stared at her in horror. *A killer,* Selena thought numbly. *I'm trapped up here with a killer.*

"Katy, please believe me," she begged, backing away from her friend. "Please believe how sorry I am."

"I do believe you," Katy replied. "But it's too late."

Selena pressed herself against the cabinet, trying to make herself disappear. "Katy, no—"

"I'm grateful to you for making it so easy," Katy said without any emotion at all. "I wasn't expecting you tonight. I thought only Danny would show up. But this makes it so much better."

"Were you the one who asked Danny to come here?"

"I'm a good actress too, Selena," Katy sneered. "I disguised my voice. I told him I was you. It was simple."

"Katy, let's go down to the stage. We can talk about everything. We can get you the help you need. I'm sure there's a way to work things out."

"No way!" Katy cried. "I've already got things worked out. It will look as if you and Danny came up here and had an accident. Everyone will think you died together. Just like the real Romeo and Juliet."

Katy lifted her heavy flashlight in the air.

She moved quickly across the small room to Selena.

30

With a low cry, Selena hurtled forward. She threw herself over Danny and scrambled to the door on the far side of the prop room.

"Please don't hurt me, Katy," she pleaded.

"Forget it," Katy replied. "There's nowhere for you to go."

She swung the flashlight.

Selena cried out as the heavy metal connected with her arm. She felt a sharp, numbing pain.

As Katy raised the flashlight to strike again, Selena jumped back. Grabbed for the doorknob.

She swung the door open.

And froze in fear.

She had forgotten where the second door led. It opened directly onto the catwalk. So high above the stage. The narrow metal walkway stretched before Selena like a tightrope.

Dizziness swept over her. She started to turn back, but Katy blocked her way.

"What's the matter, Selena?" Katy taunted. "Change your mind?"

"Katy, let me back in—"

Katy laughed. "You've always been afraid of heights, ever since we were little."

"Yes," Selena sobbed. "You know I am."

"That makes it perfect," Katy declared. "You got scared and fell off the catwalk. No one will be surprised."

"Katy, no—"

Katy swung the flashlight.

Selena dodged away. Took a step back.

Katy pulled back her arm and swung the flashlight.

Selena had no choice.

She stepped out. Onto the catwalk.

Slipped. Went over the railing.

Felt herself falling.

And realized she was plunging to her death.

31

"Noooooo!"

Uttering a desperate wail of horror, she shot up her arms. Grabbed the thin rod of a railing.

Caught it with her right hand. Held on.

Held on. Held on despite the searing pain shooting down her arm.

Held on until she could grasp the railing with her left hand, too.

Then she hoisted herself back onto the narrow walkway.

Gasping for breath, her whole body shuddering and shaking, Selena took a step back. Then another.

Katy followed, the flashlight raised in front of her.

Selena took another step. Another. Backing up

on trembling legs. Backing up. Trying not to look down. Staring at the raised flashlight in Katy's hand.

"Oh!" Selena gasped as she felt something cold against her back. She turned—and saw that she had reached the end of the catwalk. There was nowhere to go now.

Nowhere but down.

Selena's eyes were drawn to the stage below. She gasped. It was so far down. Another wave of dizziness swept over her, and she had to press her hands against the wall to keep from tumbling over.

"Scared you're going to fall?" Katy asked nastily. "You should be."

She took one more step toward Selena.

Then she swung the flashlight at Selena's head.

Selena screamed and ducked.

She lost her balance on the narrow catwalk.

And fell again.

And landed hard on her stomach, straddling the catwalk, her arms hugging it tightly.

Katy laughed.

"Please stop! Please stop! Please!" Selena begged.

"Okay," Katy agreed. "I'll stop."

Selena stared up in surprise.

Katy set down the flashlight and knelt beside

Selena. She began to pull on Selena's arms, prying them away from the catwalk.

"No!" Selena pleaded.

"Let go!" Katy ordered. She pulled harder.

Harder.

Selena closed her eyes and held on, her arms and legs wrapped tightly around the metal surface.

"You're stronger than I thought," Katy muttered. "But you won't be able to hold on if you're unconscious."

She picked up the flashlight again and raised it over her head.

Selena shut her eyes as Katy brought the flashlight down.

32

Selena waited for the pain. For the flashlight to come crashing down on her head.

She shut her eyes and waited.

Waited.

When she opened her eyes, Katy knelt over her, the flashlight raised. But now Katy was staring at the other end of the catwalk.

Selena turned her head to see Eddy at the top of the ladder.

"Put down the flashlight!" he told Katy softly.

"Go away!" Katy snarled. "This has nothing to do with you!"

"Let her go," Eddy said gently. He began to inch out on the catwalk toward the girls.

"Leave us alone!" Katy cried. She rose to her feet. "I'll take care of you, too," she muttered.

"Don't be stupid, Katy," Eddy called. "You

don't want to kill three people. You *know* you don't
want to kill Selena and me."

"You don't know what I want!" Katy replied in
an angry, trembling voice. She stood up and took a
step toward Eddy.

"Then why don't you explain?" Eddy called
to her.

"I will," Katy sneered. "If you'll come closer."

Eddy took another step toward her. Now they
were only a few feet apart.

Selena felt too afraid to move. Horrified, she
watched as Katy and Eddy faced each other. Katy
was so intent on Eddy that she seemed to have forgotten Selena.

"Put down the flashlight, Katy," Eddy
instructed her gently. "Let's go down to the stage."

"You'd like that," Katy shot back. "That way
you'd be in control. But up here, I'm in control."

Without warning, she swung the flashlight at
Eddy's head.

Selena shrieked—and Eddy ducked. He thrust
his hands out and windmilled his arms. He hit the
railing on the catwalk. Looked like he was about to
topple over it. He teetered on the edge.

It's all over, Selena thought. *Katy is going to
kill us all.*

Then she saw Eddy regain his balance. He

grabbed for the flashlight. Missed, as Katy stepped away.

With an angry grunt, she swung the flashlight again.

This time Eddy slipped. He went down with a yell, landing on the beam.

Katy swung the flashlight again.

Selena's scream drowned out the loud *thunk* as the metal flashlight found its target.

Eddy ducked back, losing his balance. He slipped off the beam. Now hanging on to it by his fingertips. His body swaying above the stage.

Katy began to chop at Eddy's hands with the flashlight. He cried out, but still held on.

He's going to die! Selena realized. *Unless I help him!*

But could she do it?

She took a deep breath, then began to crawl toward Katy.

Katy whacked at Eddy's fingers again and again.

Selena heard Eddy's cries of pain. She knew he couldn't hold on much longer.

She couldn't be careful anymore. She had to get there fast. She forced herself to stand. Without looking down, she dived toward Katy.

Katy's flashlight was raised high in the air,

ready to come down again on Eddy's hands.

Selena grabbed it.

"Let go!" Katy screeched. She tried to pull away from Selena's grasp—and lost her balance.

Selena yanked on the flashlight with all her strength. It flew out of Katy's hands and clattered onto the stage far below.

Katy grasped Selena's arms with both hands. And for a moment the two girls wrestled, teetering on the narrow walk.

Selena couldn't balance. She knew that in another moment both she and Katy would fall off, fall onto the hard stage.

And then she *was* falling, falling backward, Katy on top of her. She seemed to fall forever. Waiting for the stage to smash into her. Waiting for blackness.

"Huh?" Selena felt the catwalk under her back. A crushing weight on her stomach.

She gazed up. Katy was sprawled on top of her.

"Whooooa!" Eddy cried out as he landed on top of both of them, pinning them to the safety of the catwalk.

Selena couldn't breathe.

"Let me go!" Katy cried, struggling furiously. "Let me go!"

"Hold on, Selena," Eddy cried. He climbed to

his feet and, pulling Katy roughly up, dragged her along the catwalk. They disappeared into the prop room.

Selena stared after them, her body numb with shock. After a moment, she climbed shakily to her feet. Without Katy, the catwalk seemed safe. Walking on it seemed easy.

Slowly, she made her way to the prop room. Eddy had pulled off Danny's ropes and was using them to tie up Katy.

"How did you know I was here?" Selena asked Eddy.

"You sounded so upset on the phone, I took a guess you might come here."

"Lucky guess!" Selena cried. With a burst of emotion, she ran over and wrapped her arms around Eddy. She kissed him.

He held her close. When he pulled back, she saw the startled expression on his face. "You're not *acting* now—are you?" he demanded.

Selena pressed her face against his. "No. I'm not acting," she replied. "Thank goodness, this show is over!"

"Hey, don't say that," Eddy protested. He slid his arm around her. "This may only be Act One!"

Turn the page for a peek
at Fear Street:

RUNAWAY

WELCOME TO SHADYSIDE, the sign read.

Felicia Fletcher trudged along in the late-afternoon gloom. Dark clouds hung low and heavy, threatening to drench her again.

"Shadyside," she whispered. Never heard of it.

She wiped her hands on her jeans. It didn't help. She was soaked. Her jeans heavy with rain. Her sneakers soft and squishy. Her brown ponytail dripping icy water down her back.

Felicia peered past the WELCOME sign. A bridge spanned a swiftly flowing river. The water swept crumpled leaves and twisted branches along.

Felicia shifted the heavy red backpack on her shoulders. She pulled her navy blue baseball cap lower over her blue eyes.

Shadyside. Felicia liked the name. *Maybe I can*

be safe here, she thought. *Maybe I can start over in Shadyside.*

A lump rose in Felicia's throat. She didn't want to start over. She wanted to go home. Home where she had friends and people who cared about her.

But she couldn't. She couldn't ever go home. Not after what she did.

Don't start to cry again, Felicia, she ordered herself. *You're soaking wet as it is.* She turned and stared in the opposite direction. Should she try Shadyside—or keep moving?

Felicia wished she could forget what happened. Forget everything and everyone from the past. Start fresh.

But the memories would *never* disappear. The laboratory. The wires. The doctors.

Dr. Shanks especially.

His greasy gray beard and loud voice. Felicia remembered the first time she ever met him. They led her into the lab. The bright fluorescent lights hurt her eyes. They sat her down in a straight-backed wooden chair, the most uncomfortable chair she'd ever felt.

They crowded around her, working, working, working. A skinny man with glasses attached sticky electrodes to her temples. Green, black, red, blue, and yellow wires ran from the electrodes into a large computer terminal. The assistants barked orders back and forth.

"Trial run on module four," a gray-haired woman in a white coat called.

"Go module four," the skinny one with glasses replied. He flipped a switch, and one of the machines began a loud, rhythmic beeping. "Pulse is seventy-nine, blood pressure one-twenty."

"Is that good?" Felicia asked.

They ignored her. They always ignored her questions.

The skinny one with glasses moved a table in front of Felicia. Another assistant pushed in her chair.

"Tell Dr. Shanks that the subject is ready," the gray-haired woman ordered.

"My name is Felicia," she reminded them. "Why can't you ever use my name?"

The gray-haired woman regarded her coldly, saying nothing. She picked up a clipboard and began making notes.

"It's spelled F-E-L-I-C-I-A," Felicia grumbled.

The gray-haired woman stopped writing and stared at her.

"Did I go too fast?" Felicia asked sarcastically.

The woman set the pencil and clipboard down and left the room.

Seconds later, a bald man with a thick beard strode into the exam room, his white lab coat swishing with each step. He stood over six feet tall, with a large belly. He had a long, crooked nose, and deep-set eyes.

Angry eyes, Felicia thought. *No laughter in there. Only a big, cold, dark nothing.*

"Felicia," he said, folding his arms across his chest. "How are you today?"

"Fine."

"Fine. I am Dr. Shanks. I'm running this phase of the experiment. Unlike Dr. Cooper, I will not tolerate any sarcasm. You have to understand, Felicia. You are here to learn, but to teach as well. We need to learn from you. So you must clear your mind and concentrate. If you refuse to obey that one simple rule, you will be finished here at Ridgely College. Is that clear?"

A jolt of anger shot through Felicia. *Who does this guy think he is? They need* me *a lot more than I need* them.

Felicia gazed into Dr. Shanks's sunken eyes. He didn't turn away. He stared right back. "You need to learn to control your talents. If you don't, you will put others, and yourself, in danger."

Felicia shivered. "I understand," she finally replied.

"Fine. Let us begin." Dr. Shanks pulled a pencil from his coat pocket and placed it on the table in front of Felicia. "Move the pencil across the table, please."

"What?"

"Move the pencil across the table, please," Dr. Shanks repeated.

"I-I don't know if I can," Felicia stammered. She heard the machine's beeps increase with her heart rate. Her palms began to sweat.

"That is unacceptable," Dr. Shanks replied. "Move the pencil across the table, please."

"I can't just *do* it, you know!"

Dr. Shanks slammed his palm down on the table. "What did I just explain to you? This is not a game. This isn't even a test. This is your *life*, young lady!"

"Don't yell at me!" she screamed. "I can't help it! I'm not one of your stupid machines! You can't just turn me on and off whenever you want! Get out of my face!"

Dr. Shanks drew in a deep breath. He leaned forward on the table, placing a hand on either edge. Leaned so close Felicia could feel his breath hitting her face. Smell the mix of onions and spearmint.

"Young lady, whether you know it or not, you are blessed with one of the most remarkable talents on the face of this planet. I advise you to cooperate and concentrate. If you don't, there are more important people who are waiting to see how your abilities work. And believe me, their tests will be much more painful than this. Is that clear?"

Felicia wanted to rip the itchy electrodes off her temples and run out of the lab. *No,* she told herself. *I have to be strong. I have to try.*

Because she knew Dr. Shanks wasn't lying. Her father had told her the same thing—a long line of doctors waited to put her strange talents to the test. Shanks would not be the worst.

She stared at the pencil.

"Concentrate," he ordered.

She focused on it. The pink eraser. The yellow paint. The sharp, black point.

In the background, the beeping grew faster. Felicia's heart hammered in her chest. Full of anger. Full of fear.

Do it, she told herself. *Just do it.*

"You're not concentrating!" Dr. Shanks whispered.

But she was. Felicia hurled all her energy toward the pencil. And she felt something.

Something growing inside her. Slowly inflating. Like a balloon.

"*Concentrate,*" Dr. Shanks repeated. His voice dug deep into her brain.

Her power grew.

She pushed harder.

The machines beeped faster and faster. Felicia felt the blood rushing through her veins.

"Heart rate one-ten," came a voice from nowhere. "B.P. one-eighty."

Felicia's fingernails bit into her hands. The moisture on her palms could have been sweat—or blood.

"*Concentrate,*" came the voice.

The doctor's voice. The enemy's voice.

Kill the enemy.

The power exploded in Felicia's mind. All at once the pencil became a part of her will. And she knew *exactly* what she wanted to do with it.

The pencil wiggled. Then it slowly turned around on the table, its point turning toward Dr. Shanks.

In her mind, Felicia took a strong grip on the pencil, squeezing it with all her might. The pencil stopped wiggling and rose several inches from the table. It hovered there, as if waiting for an order.

Now, she thought. *Do it!*

She made it happen. She forced all her anger, fear, and frustration into the shaft of the pencil.

She knew it was wrong. But she couldn't help herself.

Felicia aimed it at the only target she could see—and let loose with all her might.

Felicia cried out with the effort. It felt like throwing a giant spear. *I did it!* she thought. *Yes!*

Then she watched as the pencil rocketed across the room—toward Dr. Shanks's left eye.

Twisted Tales
from
V.C. ANDREWS®

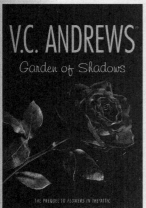

Vampires, werewolves, witches, shape-shifters—they live among us without our knowledge. The Night World is their secret society, a society with very strict rules. And falling in love breaks them all.

WELCOME TO THE NIGHT WORLD....